MAGELLANIA

Jules Verne's

MAGELLANIA

The First English-Language Edition Ever of the Original "Lost" Manuscript

INTRODUCTION BY OLIVIER DUMAS

PRESIDENT OF THE JULES VERNE SOCIETY

TRANSLATED BY BENJAMIN IVRY

WELCOME RAIN PUBLISHERS

NEW YORK

MAGELLANIA by Jules Verne
Originally published in France as *En Magellanie*

Welcome Rain Publishers would like to thank the French Ministry of Culture for its assistance with this translation.

Library of Congress CIP data available from the publisher.

Direct any inquiries to:
Welcome Rain Publishers LLC
23 West 26th Street
New York, NY 10010

ISBN 1-56649-179-7
Printed in the United States of America by
HAMILTON PRINTING COMPANY

Designed by Fritz Metsch

First Edition January 2002

1 3 5 7 9 10 8 6 4 2

PREFACE

MAGELLANIA: JULES VERNE'S POLITICAL TESTAMENT

At the time of his death, Jules Verne left behind six unpublished novels that his son Michel rewrote at his publisher's request to satisfy the tastes of the day. The first, *The Lighthouse at the End of the World,* was published in 1905, relatively unaltered. The other five underwent numerous changes that altered their essential nature. Understandably, financial considerations can dictate new happy endings, comic characters, and scientific explanations. But the novels in question lost their special qualities when they were disfigured in this way. In their original versions, the author's highly personal style may be rediscovered: his reserve, concerns, and symbolic images—everything that makes up what are seen today as his literary qualities.

Two of Jules Verne's posthumous novels have recently appeared in their original versions: *The Golden Volcano* and *The Secret of Wilhelm Storitz.* After *Magellania,* there are only two further works that remain to be published in popular editions, *The Beautiful Yellow Danube,* a merry river journey, and *The Meteor Hunt,* a satirical novel.

Before reading the texts of Jules Verne's manuscripts, we might worry about finding them mediocre or incomplete, which would have made his son's interventions providential. But after studying them, we find that this is not at all the case. By the end of his life, Jules Verne had a head start in his creativity; he had put aside a dozen finished works ready for publication, among which he would choose the ones to send to various editors or, according to the spirit of the day and the subject treated, delay their appearance.

Magellania, Jules Verne's great posthumous novel, is now offered in a previously unknown manuscript version, presented by Piero Gondolo della Riva to the Société Jules Verne, which published it in a strictly limited edition in 1987.

MAGELLANIA, THE FINAL VOYAGE "TO THE ENDS OF THE EARTH"

The novel was inspired by the mysterious death in 1891 of Archduke Johann of Austria in the waters near South America. Under the name of Jean Orth, the prince renounced his rank and sailed where he wished. In *Facing the Flag* (1896), the name of Count d'Artigas-Karraje is a nearly exact anagram for Austria (AuSTRIA/ARTIgAS). Kaw-djer, the hero of *Magellania,* is another near-anagram (two letters away) of Karraje (KARraJE/KAwdJER), and both names contain the letters "JE" for JEan d'Autriche [the French version of Johann of Austria's name]; these letters are also present in the name of Kaw-djer's boat, the *Wel-kiej.* A bandit is disguised as a nobleman in *Facing the Flag,* and a nobleman is incognito Magellania. These two facets of the same personality, positive and negative, marked the duality of that exceptional being Jean Orth, whose life and death subjugated the novelist.

Jules Verne wrote *Magellania* from October 17, 1897 to April 11, 1898, finishing it some seven years before he died. In it he denounced "those lower orders . . . who some years later would take part in the Alaskan Klondike gold rush" (ch. 15), a lode discovered on August 17, 1896, which became the subject for the novel *Volcano of Gold.* It was a dark time in the author's life: his brother had just died, his own health was deteriorating, and his mood was extremely depressed. He anxiously felt that death was approaching, as his letters show.

It is natural, then, that this new work summed up his opinions on religion and politics, and conveyed his fear of death, which he dreaded but also sometimes desired.

JULES VERNE'S MANUSCRIPT

Like all the other posthumous novels, the text, carefully corrected and modified by the author, was not given a final checking of the proofs, a gap we have attempted to fill by carefully reviewing this new edition.

Certain names of characters change in the course of the story, either from forgetfulness or carelessness. There are also the same meaningless changes in geographic names. The author sometimes tried out different names before choosing a single one. We have almost always chosen the spelling of proper names that are the first to appear, while noting their variants.

At first, the novel was entitled *Tierra del Fuego* and then, symbolically, *The Ends of the Earth,* where the book's final voyage winds up. The second chapter tells of a slow descent one night "to Hell" of a Pecherais' corpse in the silent boat of a ferryman Karroly, another Karron. The somber meditation about Kaw-djer, which serves as a meaningful and remarkably written opening for the novel, was cut by Michel Verne, no doubt because he did not understand it.

Later, after the publication of *Lighthouse at the Ends of the Earth* (1901), Jules Verne, in order to save the excellent latter title, replaced *At the Ends of the Earth* with *Magellania,* which referred to a mythical country.

SOURCES

For documentation on the Magellanian region, Verne read, among other things, two articles from the magazine *Le Tour du*

Monde: Journal of a Voyage on the Straits of Magellan by Victor de Rochas (vol. I, 1861) and *A Year at Cape Horn* by Doctor Hyades (vol. I, 1885).

Numerous details in *Magellania* originate from the Rochas text. For example, the description of the *guanaco* that begins Verne's tale:

> It was a graceful animal, with a long neck and elegant curvature, a rounded rump, nervous tapering legs, with a tawny red coat speckled with white, and a short tufted tail with very thick hair.

This is close to Rochas' description:

> It's [. . .] an elegant animal, remarkably agile, with a long neck, narrow head and flat body, long thin legs and a very fine, tawny coat spotted with white.

According to the maps that accompany these articles, "Ile Neuve" (New Island) is sometimes called "Ile Nouvelle." We understand why Verne wished to maintain the name "Ile Neuve," for it is a near anagram, one letter away, from the name of the author (NEuVE/VErNE), who made it Kaw-djer's preferred residence.

As usual, Verne provides no sources for his research, but he often introduces real characters into his work, mixing reality and fiction. Thus, in *Magellania,* Dr. Hyades' expedition aboard the *La Romanche* visits the castaways, the passengers of *The Jonathan*:

> And in 1882-1883, when the French expedition carried by the vessel *La Romanche* had anchored at the Orange Bay of Hoste Island to observe *The Venus* passing by, the few contacts that they had with the new colony left them a uniformly excellent impression. (ch. XIV)

THE WORK'S THEME

What theme did Jules Verne intend to describe in his literary testament? The story of a man, a brother of Captain Nemo, close to the author, who builds his life upon an anarchistic credo: "Neither God nor master!" Life's realities force him little by little, from adventure to adventure, to become a master himself, and the book's final pages suggest that he no longer rejects God's influence. But he lives only to maintain his "independence," without falterings or concessions. Independence is a key word in Verne's works, which recalls the last words of Captain Nemo, who dies "murmuring the word: 'Independence!'" Kaw-djer prefers to die rather than lose that independence. Symbolically, he chooses to throw himself into the ocean at the remotest point of land, "at the ends of the earth":

> Was he haunted for some time by the idea of putting an end to his life? . . . Did he tell himself that he would move ahead as long as there would be earth—which he no longer desired—under his feet, but with the decision to seek death in the waves that broke upon the farthest point of shore? [. . .] Yes! That's what he had resolved . . . (ch. VII)

The firing of a cannon by a ship in distress, *The Jonathan,* delayed the execution of this suicide. In *The Castaways of The Jonathan*—the version of the novel as transformed by Michel Verne—this explanation is withheld; therefore readers do not understand why Kaw-djer hurries in this way toward Cape Horn.

The hero repeats on several occasions his willingness to die to remain free, which is proof that he was not feeling a transitory depression:

> The thought came to him to seek in death, which is nevertheless not eternal sleep, the repose that life could not offer him! (ch. XIII)

This is an astonishing point of view for a book meant for young readers, a moving and anguished avowal that motivated the writer to delay the publication of his novel, which was so incompatible with the ideals of the Hetzel collection it was intended for.

GOLD

Despising gold was a favorite theme of Jules Verne's, used in his first novel *Five Weeks in a Balloon,* and again in *Hector Servadac,* where it was censured by Hetzel; it appears in full force in several posthumous novels: *The Meteor Hunt, The Golden Volcano,* and *Magellania.* In the latter, Verne links gold to the adventurers' poverty and ruin, without compensation:

> "Gold! . . . gold! . . . Thirst for gold!" repeated Kaw-djer. "No worse plague could ever attack our colony!" . . . (ch. XV)

By contrast, Michel Verne makes the gold prospectors sympathetic characters and leaves a productive gold mine working on Hoste Island.

KAW-DJER AND THE AUTHOR

It is difficult not to liken Kaw-djer to Jules Verne after reading in the introduction of "this enigmatic character" the following painful sentence—cut by Michel Verne:

> Life had held many disappointments for him, perhaps some ambitious dreams that never came true. (ch. IV)

This echoes a passage in a letter that Jules Verne wrote to his brother Paul:

> Myself, for whom family—my own included—has only been a source of worry and disappointment.

MICHEL VERNE'S MODIFICATIONS

Magellania was considerably developed and changed by the writer's son for its 1909 publication in two volumes (instead of a single one) and retitled, *The Castaways of The Jonathan*. The twenty added chapters and five deleted ones, plus the total rewriting of the novel, resulted in a totally different work from his father's. Indeed, when the book appeared, readers did not recognize Jules Verne's style and suspected that Michel Verne had made changes. A trial was almost necessary, but the accusers would have needed to see the manuscript of *The Castaways,* a mixture of new material from *Magellania*—crossed out and corrected—and pages exclusively written in the hand of the younger Verne.

Trying to make the novel more attractive, Michel Verne invented almost thirty characters, spiced up the action and augmented the political discussions. All of these additions distanced the book from the sole subject dealt with by the elder Verne, the evolution of a libertarian's ideas. In *The Castaways*, the author's anguish and obsessions vanished as well. Without going into all the modifications, let's focus on Michel's inadmissible betrayal of the main character, Kaw-djer.

First, Michel changed the character of Kaw-djer, who in *The Castaways* sells off the independence of Hoste Island and signs a treaty with Chile, abdicating his sovereignty. Jules Verne's stubborn hero would never have ceded his power this way. Equally shocking is Kaw-djer's use of blackmail, employing his contacts to threaten a Chilean officer, in Michel Verne's version:

> Kaw-djer said, "These rumors had some basis. If it once pleased me, and still does, to forget who I am, it would be in your interest to keep that in mind. You may realize that I can find some rather powerful allies in order to make the Chilean government consider this." (*The Castaways*, III, ch. XIV).

Jules Verne never reveals Kaw-djer's secret in *Magellania.* If he is inspired by the Archduke Johann of Austria, he doesn't admit it, since unveiling his hero's origins would have demythified him. The personality of this anarchical prince imagined by Jules Verne would never have agreed to forfeit his independence or abandon his incognito.

Even more detrimentally, Michel Verne rejects Kaw-djer's mental development. Jules Verne described the slow evolution of ideas—more theoretical than practical—of a former anarchist who found inner peace in the love of humanity and a belated, discreet, religious conversion.

In the original manuscript, Kaw-djer never expresses the desire for solitude—only, on occasion, for isolation. On the contrary, "having become the Doctor Schweitzer of Tierra del Fuego," he deliberately sought contacts, first of all with the indigenous people, and then with the entire population of Hoste Island. He is a tormented soul, but not a misanthrope. Thus, when in the last lines of *The Castaways,* Michel Verne isolates him "far from everyone, [. . .] he would live, free, alone—forever," he distorted the character created by his father. He transformed a devoted doctor into an asocial being who neither understood nor learned anything from his experiences among the people of Tierra del Fuego and Hoste Island, nor had he been changed by them.

Faced by such differences, we can understand the importance of publishing *Magellania,* Jules Verne's unknown masterpiece, which stands as an implicit confession of his political and religious feelings.

THE FIRST "LIGHTHOUSE AT THE END OF THE WORLD"

Also missing from the son's book is the father's peaceful conclusion, the illumination of the "lighthouse at the ends of the earth," whose shining rays banish the shadows of death. Michel

Verne stripped Kaw-djer of the satisfaction of celebrating this success, this presence of the mysteries of eternal life.

Instead of Michel Verne's pessimistic ending, the original one from *Magellania* is astonishing in its feeling of alleviation of suffering. Perhaps the author really did find an answer to his anguish in God. He built up, with us all and death as witnesses, the lighthouse of his works. He illuminated the world as a witness to the present and perhaps as a guardian of the future. This symbolic lighthouse, which was already present on the back of Hetzel's packing boxes, shone upon the long series of Jules Verne's "Extraordinary Voyages."

—Olivier Dumas
President, the Jules Verne Society

MAGELLANIA

I

THE GUANACO

It was a graceful animal, with a long neck, elegant curvature, rounded rump, and nervous tapering legs with a tawny, white-speckled red coat, and a short, tufted, thick-haired tail. In the countryside it was called the *guanaco,* or *guanaque.* Seen from afar, these ruminants were often mistaken for mounted horses. Several travelers, deceived by this appearance, thought they were seeing a whole band of horsemen racing across the interminable [plains] of the region, in a given formation.

The guanaco was alone, a quarter of a mile behind the coastline. He had just paused, with a certain defiance, on the crest of a hillock in the middle of a vast prairie in which rushes brushed against one another noisily and hurled their sharp points between the clumps of prickly plants. With his snout turned to the wind, he breathed in the emanations that a light breeze brought from the east. With an attentive, nervous eye, he was wary of some kind of surprise. Pivoting with his ears standing up, he listened, and would have taken flight at the least suspicious noise. No doubt a bullet might strike this defiant animal if a hunter had a long-range gun, or an arrow, if a bowman hid behind a bush or rock. But rarely does a lasso manage to grip a guanaco in one of its loops. Thanks to extraordinary agility and speed faster than a horse's, it rapidly slips away and is out of reach after a few quick leaps.

The plain's surface is not uniformly flat in the part overlooked by the hillock. Here and there, the soil was raised into shoulders of ground, swellings that the stormy, massive rains had left behind after furrowing the earth. Along one of these shoulders, at less than a dozen steps from the hillock, crept an Indian, an indigenous dweller whom the guanaco did not notice. The half-naked man was clothed in shreds of animal fur. Lithe as a snake, he crawled silently, threading his way among the high grasses, in order to get close to the prey he was after, which would have fled at the slightest alert. However, the guanaco started to show some signs of worry, and perceive the threat of imminent danger.

Indeed, a strap was soon hurled, whistling through the air. Thrown from a good distance away, the lasso uncoiled toward the animal, and the long strap, pulled by the stone ball fixed at its tip, did not reach the guanaco's head, but slipped over his rump, not catching him.

The attempt had failed. The animal, after a sharp sidestep, ran away at full speed. When the Indian arrived at the top of the hillock, he only saw it for an instant as it disappeared behind a solid mass of trees bordering that side of the plain.

The guanaco was no longer in danger, but now the native man was threatened.

Having wound up the lasso, the end of which was attached to his belt, he was ready to climb down, when suddenly a furious roaring burst out a few steps away from him.

Almost immediately, a wild animal leapt rapidly, crashed down at his feet, got up again, and jumped at his throat.

It was a jaguar, one of the tigers of the Americas, smaller than its Asian relative, but whose attack is equally fearsome. A jaguar, of the genus feline, measures between four and five feet from head to tail, with a grayish yellow pelt on its back, marbled on the neck and sides with black spots with lighter centers, like the pupils of an eye.

The native man leapt violently to one side. He felt the power and ferocity of this animal, whose claws were tearing at his chest, and whose teeth were strangling him with a single blow from its jaws. Unfortunately, while backing up, he stumbled and stretched out at full length. He was lost, having no other weapon than a sort of knife, made from a much-tapered seal bone, which he managed to pull out of his belt.

Raising his hand high when the animal leapt upon him, he struck it with the knife, insufficient against such a terrifying adversary. The latter took a step backward, and he hoped to be able to get up and strike a better defensive position. He didn't have time. The slightly wounded jaguar jumped again, and his claws knocked the man down to the ground.

At this moment, the sharp retort of a rifle resounded, and the jaguar fell, struck down by a bullet through the heart.

Some thin white smoke was seen atop one of the cliff's rocks, one hundred feet away. Standing on this rock was a man, with a rifle still on his shoulder. Seeing that it wouldn't be necessary to fire a second time, he lowered the rifle, uncocked it, put it under his arm, and turning around, gazed toward the south.

In this direction, below the rocky cliff, lay a wide stretch of sea.

The man shouted out, leaning forward, adding some words with a guttural intonation, accentuated by the double consonant K.

However, he was not a native. He seemed to be a European or American type. Although strongly sunburnt, his skin was not brown. Nor did he have the race's flat nose and deep sunken eye sockets, high cheekbones, low receding forehead, and small eyes. On the contrary, his forehead was high, marked with the many lines of a thinking man, and his physiognomy was intelligent. He had close-cropped hair, graying like his beard, which natives of this country almost entirely lack.

The individual's age might be somewhere between forty and fifty, give or take a decade. He was tall and fit, with indestructible good health. Everything about him bespoke energy, which sometimes took the explosive form of anger. Great muscular power distinguished him. His face was marked with gravity, a little like the gravity of the American Indian, and his entire being exuded pride, quite different from the pride of egoists who are in love with themselves. This gave him a true nobility of gesture and stance.

After the first shout from the top of the cliff, there came a second, which must have been a call to a person whose name was of native origin:

"Karroly . . . Karroly!"

A minute later this Karroly appeared, through a gap in the cliff, much widened at its crest and narrowed at the base, which extended to a yellowish beach strewn with black stones.

He was certainly an Indian, a very different type from the white man who had just made his entrance on the scene with such splendid gunfire.

He was about thirty-five to forty years old, five and a half feet tall, strongly muscled, with wide shoulders, a powerful torso, and a large square head on a well-developed neck, very brown skin, very black eyes, piercing eyes under thin eyebrows, with a few reddish hairs in the guise of a beard. In fact, it might be fair to say that in this member of an inferior race, there were as many animal characteristics as human ones, but they were gentle and caressing animal ways. He had nothing of the wild animal in him, but rather the physiognomy of a good and faithful dog, like a courageous Newfoundland dog, who can become man's friend and not just his companion. Indeed, he came at the sound of his name, like one of those devoted animals, to rub himself against the master whose hand gripped his own.

A few words were exchanged in low voices between these two in the native language mentioned above, with shallow gasps that seemed to occur in half of the words spoken. Then both men went toward the spot where the wounded man lay on the soil near the dead jaguar.

The victim had lost consciousness. Blood still flowed in thin streams from his chest, which had been lacerated by the beast's claws, and reddened the soil. However, although his eyes were closed, he reopened them when he felt a hand leaning on his shoulder and pushing aside his coarse animal skin garment, under which several other wounds were bleeding.

Observing the man who hastened to give him first aid, he doubtless recognized him, for his eyes lit up with a feeble glint, and his discolored lips formed this name:

"Kaw-djer . . . Kaw-djer! . . ."

This word, which means friend or benefactor in the native language, evidently applied to the white man, for he made an affirmative sign. No doubt the native felt reassured by Kaw-djer's presence. He knew that he wasn't in the hands of a witch doctor, a caster of spells, or potion sellers known as "yakamouches," massage therapists who travel from tribe to tribe and richly deserve the bad reception they sometimes receive.

But when the injured man put his hand to his mouth, after having painfully raised it to the heavens, and exhaled weakly, as if to ask if his soul would fly away, Kaw-djer, who had examined his wounds, looked away sadly.

The native man's eyes had closed again and he didn't see this meaningful movement. Otherwise, while the bandaging went on, he did not emit a single cry of pain.

After having rapidly climbed down the cliff again, Karroly returned with a game bag that contained a medical instrument case and some flasks of sap from certain local plants. While he held the injured man's head on his knees, Kaw-djer uncovered his chest, washed his wounds with a little water that flowed down from the hillock, stanched the flow of the last drops of blood, and placing some shredded swabs soaked with ointment from one of the flasks on the wounds, compressing them. Then, taking off the woolen belt that girded his loins, he wrapped it around the native's chest to keep the bandages in place.

Surely Kaw-djer did not believe that the Indian would survive, even after the medical care he had received. There was no remedy that could heal the torn flesh, which extended to the abdominal organs and lungs. But in no event would he abandon the unfortunate man, so long as he retained a single breath of life. He would bring the man back to the campground he had left, for several days perhaps, in order to hunt guanacos, nandus, and vicunas. The native was weakened by blood loss, and his wounds might reopen at the slightest movement. Could he survive the strain of travel, if long distances were involved?

Since the Indian's eyes had just reopened, Karroly asked him:

"Where is the tribe?"

"There . . . there . . ." he answered, pointing to the east.

Kaw-djer noted, "That must be four or five miles from here, along the banks of the canal, the Wallah campground whose fires we noticed at night."

Karroly nodded his head yes.

Kaw-djer added, "It's only four o'clock, but the tide will rise soon and we won't get to Wallah before sunrise."

"Yes," said Karroly, lifting his arm, "the breeze is blowing from the west, yet . . ."

"A weak breeze that will die down in the evening," replied Kaw-djer. "Nevertheless, the current will be with us, up to Picton Island."

Karroly was ready to leave.

"Let's get the Indian on his feet again," said Kaw-djer, "and maybe he can make it down as far as the beach."

The wounded man, held up by Karroly, tried to remain standing, but his knees buckled and he fainted. It was necessary to carry him in their arms.

They had about six hundred feet to cross in order to get to the foot of the cliff. As for the jaguar, the price of his fur assured that Karroly would be back to get him after the Indian was brought down to the beach.

The jaguar was indeed a superb animal whose body would sell at a high price to foreign traffickers. In this country, skins were the main commercial objects, and there was frequent business with fur dealers.

The two men carried the injured native. They took hold of him, one by the legs, and the other by the shoulders. Thanks to their vigor, the body did not weigh them down too much. Having skirted the base of the hillock, they moved along the shoulder of soil and headed toward the beach, taking little steps in order to avoid jolts. From time to time, they stopped when a loud groan was heard from their burden. It was better to move him along slowly. There was no rush, since the Wallah campground could not be reached before dawn.

At this time of year, in May, which corresponds to November in the northern hemisphere, the sun had not disappeared under the horizon. The western mountains did not hide it yet, and that day it was setting in a clear sky, barely veiled by mists in the lower zones.

It took nearly fifteen minutes to reach the bottom of the cliff, at the flaring of the rift that extended between the rocks up to the gap. This steep slope, strewn with gleaming pebbles and sharp flints, required serious attention to avoid collisions or falls.

Kaw-djer paused before confronting it, and the Indian was placed on the ground, his back pressing against the slope. Had his wounds reopened? Had any jostling disturbed the bandages? Was the injured man still breathing? One might doubt it, given the frightful pallor of his face, pale despite the dark coloring of his forehead and cheeks.

Karroly looked at him and believed that he was dead, and made the same gesture that the Indian had done when Kaw-djer arrived. His hand went to his mouth, then pointed to heaven, and he let out a soft exhaling sound.

Kaw-djer kneeled beside the injured man, leaned over his chest, and listened for his heartbeat. His heart was beating, an almost imperceptible palpitation, but nonetheless beating.

"Let's wait," said Kaw-djer. Pulling some flasks from his game bag, he poured a few drops of a tonic for the Indian, whose chilled cheeks regained a little warmth.

During this pause, Karroly returned to the hillock in order to bring the jaguar's body to the cliff's edge, where he would return to collect it. The bullet had not damaged the animal skin, making a barely visible hole on the animal's left side, and the blood had not stained it at all. The merchants, who went from tribe to tribe to obtain furs, would buy it for a good price, whether in piastres, tobacco, or other objects of exchange. Karroly lifted up the animal, turned around, placed it on his back, and as fit as he was, struggled to carry it. Then he returned toward the cliff, with the beast's long tail sweeping along the ground.

Kaw-djer, very worried, barely cast a glance at the animal. One last time, he sounded the Indian's chest, and after rising, still did not give Karroly the order to start off again. On the contrary, he took a few steps toward the ridge, lifting himself onto one of the highest rocks that overlooked it, and gazed out over all points of the horizon. It was as if before climbing down, he could not resist observing the vast region that stretched out before him, to fill his spirit with these last impressions, and glide over the strange territories embraced within the double boundaries of earth and sea.

The land beneath was divided into the coastline's haphazard confusion, in which blackish rocks contrasted with the yellow sand of the beach. They marked the border of a canal that was several leagues wide, whose opposite bank blurred into vague outlines, and which was indented in arms of the sea as far as the eye could follow. To the east, the canal was bordered on its southern side by a sprinkling of islands and islets, whose high relief broke off in the distant sky. To the north, glaciers lined up as far as the eye could see, and to the south stretched the limitless ocean.

The source and issue of the canal could not be seen either to the east or west. Therefore it was impossible to observe either of the two extremities of the coastline, along which the high and massive cliff ran.

To the north, prairies and plains stretched interminably, streaked with a few rivers that flowed through the vast lonely terrain, and whose outpourings occurred either in breaks through the gap in tumultuous torrents, or from atop the crest line, in resounding waterfalls. The varied rounded forms of a mountain chain appeared at a distance of five or six leagues against a background of still-dazzling light, at the peripheral line of the sky. Here and there on the surface of the immense pampas lay some islets of greenery, thick forests in which no village could be found. Their blackish summits grew purple from the rays of the setting sun, which the screen of western mountains would soon cover.

On the other side, the countryside's profile was accentuated in larger proportions. Straight above the seashore, the cliffs extended endlessly in successive levels, and a dozen leagues farther away, abruptly leapt into high peaks, which became lost in the higher regions of the sky. One of these domes with a round top, in the shape of a balloon, was the closest one, and across this rarefied, acute, and transparent atmosphere, seemed to be only a short distance away. Neither its volume nor altitude were comparable to the mountains which stood out from the lateral masses, leaning against the enormous frame of the orographical system: mountains topped with snow, veneered with dazzling glaciers, high enough to point up to the frigid loftiness of space, and whose tips pierced the highest clouds at over six thousand feet above sea level.

This countryside's appearance gave the impression that it was uninhabitable. Deserted, yes, but abandoned, no! No doubt it was lived in by Indians from the same race as the wounded man, sometimes settled, sometimes migratory, who traveled across the forests and plains, feeding on game, fish, roots, and fruits, and living in ajoupas made of branches and dirt, or camping in animal-skin tents held in place by stakes.

Along the surface of the lengthy canal, the same solitude was felt. No small craft, tree-bark dinghy, or dugout canoe with a sail was in sight. As far as the eye could see, there were no islands or islets, no demarcation of seashore, and no cliff jutting out, with no smoke rising that might denote a human presence.

Apart from the guanaco that escaped from the Indian's lasso, and the jaguar that Kaw-djer's bullet killed, no quadruped, whether wild beast or ruminant, was present as a sign of animal life in this region, although the beaches were used for sporting about by amphibians, several pairs of wader birds pecked at the rocks for kelp, and bands of shrill birds built their nests in holes in the cliff.

For a moment, a line of nandus rode on the northern pampas, those ostriches which are smaller than their relatives in Asia and Africa, but no less wild and quick. Then several stifled wailings troubled the dismal solitude. Some pairs of surprisingly lithe sea lions had managed to climb the steepest escarpments of the cliff, to arrive at the crest, where wolves lay in ambush in order to catch them by surprise.

Albatrosses as white as swans passed by in more numerous troops in the air than on the water's surface or the ground, whistling, cheeping, and filling the air with the rustle of their wide wings, as well as skuas with long cylindrical beaks, which are tyrannical to aquatic species, long-tailed cormorants, and other web-footed birds that sported across the last rays of sunlight, less noisily at the setting of the radiant star than when the disc reappears over the horizon.

At that moment just before twilight, a time that is always marked by a certain sadness, Kaw-djer, standing on a high rock motionless as a statue, perceived none of these impressions. His eyes relentlessly scanned the immensity of land and sea. He barely blinked, and perhaps accustomed to the spectacle of this calm, lonely place, he looked more inside himself than outside. It seemed as if he departed into his own domain, from which no force could remove him . . .

For several minutes he remained this way, caressed by the dying breeze without budging a muscle of his face, nor did any gesture break his pensive immobility.

Then his arms, which had been over his chest, uncrossed, and his eyes looked first at the ground, then at the heavens, and from his lips came these words, which doubtless contained a summing-up of his mysterious life:

"No . . . Neither God nor master!"

II

ALONG THE CANAL

Kaw-djer turned to Karroly and told him in Indian language:

"It will take two of us to carry the Indian to the longboat without jostling him. Leave the jaguar here, and you'll come back to get it later."

Indeed, the most difficult challenge now was to follow the gap in the cliff that ended in the beach, whose incline required crawling to climb it and sliding to get down. The injured man was still unconscious, and his chest rose in weak, irregular breathing. However, Kaw-djer vowed to bring him back to the Wallah campground, dead or alive.

He said, "His family will see him one last time, even if it will just be a dead body."

They began the descent with caution and dexterity in order to avoid falling. Karroly used extraordinary strength to hold himself and the body up against rock ledges, as Kaw-djer led the way. He loosened a scree of stones that almost made them both drop. It took them fully ten minutes to reach the narrowing of the gap and emerge onto the beach.

There they paused again, and Karroly went to collect the jaguar's body—with difficulty and some damage to the fur—which he brought to the foot of the cliff.

When he stepped onto the beach, Kaw-djer, who was listening to the Indian's heart, rose up silently.

The injured man was taken across the beach battered with little rocks and strewn with countless seashells.

At the beach's edge, a longboat was gently swaying at the end of its moorings, following the undertow of the rising sea. It was a solidly built small craft with two masts, different from native dugout canoes, which have a covered upper deck from the stem to the step of the mast in the stern. Its rigging recalled that of Breton sardine boats, whose square foresail, plated on a boom, was kept rigid on its stay, and could serve as the jib. Better than native dinghies, with their sails made of matting, outriggers, and clutter, this longboat could venture beyond the canal into channels that connected it to the sea. The longboat contained a half-dozen vicuna and guanaco skins, gathered during their travels.

The Indian was put on board, placed beneath the upper deck, and stretched out on a bed of dried grass without regaining consciousness.

Karroly returned to the foot of the cliff, loaded the jaguar on his back and placed it in the back of the longboat, whose two sails were tightly hoisted. A few puffs of air moved it away from the beach, and when it was asail, the name *Wel-kiej* could be read on its stern, which is the word for seagull in native language.

It was almost five o'clock, and for six more hours, the ebb tide would draw the canal waters to the east. The longboat, taken up in the current, kept at a cable length [approximately 200 meters] from the left bank. It slipped away quickly, thanks to what remained of the northwestern wind on these tranquil waters, like those of a lake sheltered by waterside hills. Sometimes the sails filled out when the wind ran in intermittent bursts through some of the cliff's wide anfractuosities. Then the *Wel-kiej* took on a stronger list, and Karroly, who was steering, stood ready to unfurl the mainsail sheet, and to turn the helm to the wind, if need be. But as noted, the breeze grew gentler with the sunset, and a half hour later, the longboat would only have the current on its side.

Little by little, the cliff's outline lowered as it extended toward the east, interrupted by wide notches. After the arid rocks came the green plains, wide prairies, and dense forests. The coves, mostly irrigated from the canal's tributary rivers, grew larger as they added to the coast's indentations.

Kaw-djer and Karroly did not exchange a single word. From time to time, the former bent down toward the upper deck, looked at the Indian, feeling his chest, which barely moved with his last gasps of life, and tried to revive him by moistening his pale lips with a few drops of tonic. Then, he regained his place in the stern, and remained wrapped in a silence that his companion did not try in any way to break.

The *Wel-kiej,* driven by the ebb tide, continued its descent until eight o'clock in the evening. The moon, in its first quarter, had just disappeared, after the sun. The night was dark. It was necessary to moor the longboat in a place sheltered from rocks, for the rising tide would shortly make itself felt.

Karroly headed for a narrow cove, at the bottom of a promontory, whose lowest stratum dipped into the undertow's lapping waves. The small craft, berthed on its base, was attached by a grappling iron. Its two sails were brailed up and hung down the masts, and the evening meal was prepared.

Nothing could be simpler. Karroly collected a few armfuls of dried wood that was scattered on the seashore, built a fireplace between two rocks, and lit it. The menu for this meal consisted of several fish caught that morning, including some small-size loaches, leftovers of a haunch of guanaco, duck eggs hardboiled under the ashes, some biscuits that the longboat had on supply; and to drink, sweet water from a neighboring creek, with a bit of rum added. Then, Karroly washed the silverware and cookware that had been used, putting them back into the equipment trunk on board, and after saying a warm good night to Kaw-djer, and a handshake, he went to stretch out on the forward part of the upper deck, where he quickly fell asleep.

A dark and silent night, although the sky was dotted with stars, among which shone the diamonds of the Southern Cross constellation, midway between the horizon and zenith. There was no sound apart from the last flutterings of the surge against the pebbles. The aquatic birds had already returned to their nests. No moonbeams broke the darkness of the area, neither at the surface of the grasslands nor across the depths of the distant forests. A single person remained awake amid this scene of nature plunged into sleep.

Kaw-djer was sitting in the longboat's stern, his arm leaning against the planking, his legs protected by a blanket against the night's cold. He doubtless would stay in that position, wrapped up in his thoughts, until the tide returned six hours later, allowing him to continue on his way.

However, after some moments, he was distracted from his musing, and stood up, listening and looking around him, thinking he had heard some noise, either from the shore or the sea. Then, realizing his mistake, he sat down again, pulled the blanket over his knees, and returned to his meditative stillness.

He may have dozed off until two o'clock in the morning, when he stood up at the same moment that Karroly did. The longboat's shaking, as it swung at anchor, had just awakened them.

"The ebb tide . . . " said Karroly.

"Let's go," answered Kaw-djer.

And before anything else, he went toward the upper deck.

The Indian was breathing so weakly that it was necessary to put one's ears to his lips to make sure that there was still life in him.

The wind rose on the slack tide—a light and favorable land breeze. The *Wel-kiej* might therefore reach that Wallah campground they were heading toward, by going down the canal.

They navigated silently along the water's surface, mottled by a few reverberations, but still almost entirely somnolent. The longboat maintained its route at a few hundred feet from the banks, whose outlines first began to be vaguely sketched to the east against the slightly brighter background of the sky. Two or three fires threw blurred light upon the shadows, from campgrounds that Kaw-djer doubtless would have visited according to his custom had it been day and had he not been in a hurry to get to his destination. Here and there, sheltered by tents, Indian families rested, protected against attack from wild animals by these homes, which were watched all night.

The hours flowed by, and the wind, which grew cooler as dawn approached, made the small craft pick up speed, with its sails trembling slightly along their bolt ropes.

Finally, an imperceptible glimmer began to color the sea's horizon in the west. First some vapors grew purple, then dissipated as they lowered, as if they had faded away in front of an oven's mouth. Soon the zenith appeared mottled with little shining spots, and in back, an array of colors from red to white spread out their elusive hues. The sun suddenly appeared and as often occurs during the morning hours, a shiver of golden rays ran across the fluttering surface of the sea.

It was six o'clock. The *Wel-kiej* had reached the edge of the canal, marked by a collection of scattered islets upon which penguins slapped the air with their stumpy wings. Three-quarters of the way along the southern perimeter was the infinite ocean, encircled with light from the sun's oblique rays. Visible to the north was a low, quite wide coastline with flat beaches. Around two to three miles behind these beaches stood beechwood forests, whose branches horizontally stretched out vast parasols of delicate green. The coast went as far as the eye could see, rising a little toward the northeast, and at some twenty leagues further along, its outermost point could be found, sharp as a billhook, which bent down into the Atlantic Ocean.

At this spot, tents stood in no particular arrangement, held in place by stakes, beside a stream, whose bed was filled with clear water that moved sinuously between the aromatic winterias and common barberries. Many pairs of dogs gamboled around, and their loud barks announced the longboat's arrival. Nearby, on the bare prairie, some small and seemingly sickly horses were grazing.

Here and there, thin streams of smoke emerged from the tents' cones and also from the leafy rooftops of five or six ajoupas, set up on the nearby shore to the right, whose farthest trees dipped their roots into the sea.

As soon as the *Wel-kiej* was spied, it was identified, and sixty men and women dressed in native garb, covered with blankets of guanaco hair, came out of the tents and rushed to the beach. A crowd of half-naked children ran after them, seeming not to mind the cold, despite the nippy breeze.

Certainly Kaw-djer would be welcome in the Wallah campground. He was a familiar visitor to the Indian families, the migrant or settled tribes, whether in the country's interior or on the banks of the canal.

When the small craft was moored in back of a narrow cove at the river's mouth, Karroly threw the grapnel ashore, and a native hurriedly drove it into the sand. The sails were lowered and Kaw-djer quickly stepped off.

They hurried around him, shaking his hand. The Indians' welcome showed a warm friendliness, mixed with gratitude. They must have received much help from Kaw-djer. They were the ones who gave this name meaning benefactor to the stranger who doubtless came from some far-off land overseas.

With one and then another, he spoke in their language. He followed several into their tents and ajoupas, a woman leading him to her sick child whom he examined, giving him a few mouthfuls of tonic from his traveling pharmacy. The same thing happened at several of these families' homes, and the mothers thanked him effusively, reassured and consoled by his presence. Soon he no longer knew who to listen to first. Each one needed him and demanded his care. They wanted to lead him away to make a general visit of the campground, as if they had expected him for many months. Limited to their own resources, the Indians seemed to want to stock up on good deeds until his next visit.

The campground, which numbered around thirty families, or almost a tribe, was not under the authority of a chief. At least, no such tent stood apart by any particular appearance. Not one of these natives had presented himself to Kaw-djer as possessing that rank. These Indians lived communally, after all.

It was not to visit the tribe's most important person—since they didn't have one—that Kaw-djer headed for one of the ajoupas built near the forest.

Respecting a gesture that he made, the Indians let him go there alone. He entered, and a few minutes later, he came out. Two women followed him, one aged around fifty but seeming older than her years, with a deeply wrinkled face and weary body, while the other was of medium height, at most twenty years old, with attractive, regular features, wearing a bead necklace and shell bracelets on her arms.

The latter woman, dragging herself more than walking, held a little child by the hand. She lacked the smiling face, the joyous physiognomy of the other Indians of the Wallah campground. Overwhelmed with grief, she expressed her acute pain through her wailing and crying.

Kaw-djer returned to the longboat. Karroly had not yet come ashore. When he was given the word, he leaned over toward the upper deck and pulled out the Indian's body.

The injured man never regained consciousness. Two hours earlier, he had given his last gasp, despite the medical care he had received. On his face, twisted into a final spasm, was death's lividness.

As soon as the body was placed on the bank, the two women—one was the dead man's mother, the other his wife—kneeled down, throwing themselves at him as they burst into sobs.

The campground's natives gathered around them. They all knew the man who had left the day before with his bow, arrows, and lasso to hunt the guanaco across the western plains, the one that the *Wel-kiej* had just brought back home dead to his mother, wife, and child.

Then Kaw-djer told the tale of what happened in native language, which he spoke with extreme facility. He indicated precisely where on the coastline the encounter took place, under what conditions his intervention occurred, how the jaguar was struck by a bullet but too late, and how its claws had torn into the Indian's chest, wounding him fatally.

When the animal was taken off board, following orders given to Karroly, the dead man's companions dragged it around with furious shouts, heaping abuse on it and throwing stones at it, while the two kneeling women were engulfed in their suffering.

Kaw-djer allowed these feelings of revenge to be expressed, even though Karroly showed his disapproval of the damage to the animal's pelt.

The young woman, who remained close to her husband's body, leaned over him. She half-opened his mouth, and it looked as if she were collecting a last gasp in order to spread it out into space. She seemed to be taking his soul from its mortal casing, and watching it fly off to the sky.

Kaw-djer moved back a few steps, turning his head away.

Then the widow, with a sort of rhythmic arm movement, began singing a mournful song, punctuated by sobs marked by indescribable sorrow.

Thus did the natives have an intuition about life after death, a feeling about returning to a higher world after life. Was the divinity they worshiped one of those pagan idols that savage peoples often adore? On the contrary, they had renounced their superstitions and former practices and converted to the teachings of the Christian religion, whose influence never stopped growing due to the efforts of missionaries who spread out to the remotest lands of the Atlantic and Pacific.

If they had been wrenched away from atavistic idolatries, if the Faith had been propagated as far as them, it could not have been because of Kaw-djer. He was a benefactor who visited them but was no apostle. We recall the atheistic and anarchic motto that he spoke the night before, standing on the crest of the cliff, when his eyes scoured the surrounding region.

No, it wouldn't be this white man of European or American

origin—we don't know which—who would come to say a final prayer over the Indian's body and plant a cross over his grave.

Now that his visit to the Wallah campground was over, he was going to reembark on the longboat and take to the sea, leaving it to the natives to prepare the necessary funeral, when some excitement started on the forest's edge.

A dozen Indians, who had just climbed the left bank of the creek, saw two men appear, pausing for a moment at the first line of trees.

These men were whites who belonged to the Apostolic missions. One was over fifty years old, with graying hair and beard. The other was younger by a few years. Both wore wide-brimmed hats and long ecclesiastical garments.

These missionaries were from Canada and belonged to the Catholic establishment set up in this land at the ends of the earth. Here they struggled courageously and successfully against the influence of clergymen from diverse Protestant, Methodist, and Wesleyan sects, who were so fierce in their propaganda campaigns.

There are a good number of ardent preachers in missions on neighboring islands owned by Great Britain. These establishments own a few little steamboats with which they did a sort of coastal trading in religion and also merchandise. They exported grain, livestock, and cargoes of Bibles, in English as well as in native language. They even took care to adapt the holy book's texts to agree with the circumstances and peculiarities of a rigorous winter climate, by threatening fishermen with a special hell, in which instead of being burned by eternal fire, the damned are sentenced to torture by cold so extreme that the Fahrenheit thermometer is unable to measure its descent below the freezing point.

At that moment, Kaw-djer was about to step aboard the longboat, while Karroly was bringing back the jaguar's mistreated body. He turned and scanned the forest's edge while preparing to cast off, but after a short hesitation he stopped and remained on the beach.

As soon as the missionaries had been noticed by the natives, the latter hurried to meet them and welcomed them as they had Kaw-djer, with equal gratitude and friendliness. It wasn't the first time that Fathers Athanase and Severin had visited the Wallah campground, or the other small tribes sparsely present on the surface of these territories. Each year their evangelical tours led them from tribe to tribe, whether to the country's interior, along the canal, or in neighboring islands. By their Canadian origin, these priests had French blood mixed with blood from the Saxon race, and they bravely battled with clergymen over the conquest of these regions.

The two missionaries had met Kaw-djer on several occasions. Although they did for the soul what he did for the body, fulfilling their responsibilities with the same zeal and charity as he did, they had failed to broach the mysterious character's incognito.

At any rate, the latter showed no intention of making contact with them when they approached. Given his free-thinking beliefs and the disdain he professed for all religious practices, he was unable to welcome the missionaries' intervention.

However, the fathers joined the two women who were still kneeling near the dead body. The elder priest leaned over the body. He quickly learned what Kaw-djer had told them, and of the burden he had assumed by bringing the Indian's body back to his mother, wife, and child. It behooved them, he felt, to thank him for doing so.

So Father Athanase rose up and went to the longboat, stopped in front of Kaw-djer and spoke to him in English, in which they were both fluent, saying:

"You did everything you could for this poor man. We know how charitable you are . . . And what devotion you are capable of toward these poor natives . . ."

Kaw-djer made a gesture, showing that his actions did not deserve that much praise.

All he said was, "I only did my duty."

The father replied, "Since you have done your duty, sir, then you'll understand that we also want to do ours!"

And, returning next to the body, he knelt down in prayer for the repose of the dead man's soul. The Indian, a Christian convert, was given a Christian burial.

The body was lifted from the ground and carried by hand. His mother, wife, and other tribeswomen followed. The two missionaries stood at the head of the funeral cortège holding crucifixes, and reciting final prayers, they went toward the woods where a grave sheltered by trees would be dug.

Kaw-djer and Karroly embarked, and the *Wel-kiej*, with its sails high, helped by a gentle northwestern breeze, headed toward the open sea.

III

MAGELLANIA

The events just recounted took place on the southern coast of Tierra del Fuego.

Modern geographers use the name Magellania to include the domain of islands and islets between the Atlantic and Pacific Oceans, at the southernmost tip of the American continent. The continent's remotest land mass, Patagonia, is prolonged by two vast peninsulas—King William Island and Brunswick—ending with one of the latter's capes, called Cape Froward. This domain is made up of everything that isn't directly attached to Patagonian territory, everything that is separated from it by the Straits of Magellan, justly named after the illustrious sixteenth-century Portuguese seafarer.

Magellania is formed by the combination of Tierra del Fuego; Desolation Bay; the islands of Clarence, Hoste, and Navarin; the Cape Horn Archipelago; as well as Grevy, Wollaston, Freycinet, Hermitte, Herschell, and Deceit Islands; and numerous islets and barrier reefs, all grouped at the limits of the inhabited world.

This domain extends over a surface of fifty thousand kilometers, of which approximately twenty thousand make up the Fuegian region, or Tierra del Fuego.

To follow the vicissitudes of this story to good purpose, one must know how Magellania was discovered, and its geographical makeup, to learn what ties link it to the republics of Argentina and Chile.

As we know, almost a century separated the surveying of the Straits of Magellan in 1520 and Cape Horn (or Hoorn) in 1610. The Portuguese seafarer had skirted round the American continent's extreme point, before Willem Schouten, the Dutch seaman, overtook the famous Cape, on which he imposed the name of his native town.

From this fact we may conclude that when Magellan crossed the straits between America and Magellania from east to west, it could be believed that a new American continent, as wide as the existing one, extended to the farthest heights of the Antarctic polar region.

But in reality, it was limited to Tierra del Fuego and its large and small island dependencies, of which the most distant one leads up to Cape Horn.

As a consequence of this geographical arrangement, until the year 1881, when the present tale begins, no country seemed to have had the right to claim this part of the New World, as was accurately stated by one of the companions of Dumont d'Urville in the voyage of *The Astrolabe* and *The Zélée* in the Straits of Magellan. Not a single one, not even neighboring countries like Chile and the Argentinean republic, which fought over the Patagonian territories. Magellania belonged to no one, and the colonies were founded while maintaining full independence. Even England, at [. . .] leagues to the east, which had put its rapacious hand on the Falklands or Malvinas as early as 1771, never claimed ownership of any islands in the Magellanic Archipelago.

That situation is important to describe before recounting the events that intimately involve this story's hero.

The Straits of Magellan open onto the Atlantic Ocean between the Cape des Vierges and the Cape Espiritu-Santo, then widen to form two vast bays, Possession Bay to the north and Lomas Bay to the south, and squeeze to form the bottleneck of the first narrows.

On October 21, 1520, Magellan's fleet crossed the interior sea. The Portuguese seafarer sent three ships ahead to explore. The first, with its crew in mutiny after being irresistibly pushed back by the currents, had to return to Europe. The second, perturbed by low waters in a canal farther to the southeast, and almost running aground on the reefs, gave up its quest.

Luck allowed the third, commanded by Magellan himself, to cross the straits. During twenty-two days of sailing on the surface of the deep canal, he followed a path between the banks of Patagonia and Tierra del Fuego. That's the name given to this remote portion of the American continent, because its inhabitants, called Patagonians, or "men with large feet," had long shoes made from guanaco skins. As for Tierra del Fuego (Land of Fire), it received this name, and its natives were called Fuegians, because a number of fires shone on its surface. On both sides of the straits were green prairies, dense forests, an entire system of sweet-water rivers, and as the ships moved westerly, high snow-covered mountains.

Finally Magellan disembogued at an unknown ocean so calm that it deserved the name Pacific, although not before bravely conquering mighty obstacles and fighting against almost continually contrary winds.

Thus was the channel crossed. It only remained to follow the notable seaman's path—dangerous sailing in short, and particularly difficult for sailing ships, especially when they tried to advance from east to west against the straits' prevailing winds.

Three years later, Magellan's successor, Captain Ladrilleros, acting under orders from the Chilean governor Gargie de Mendoza, had to turn back when faced by bad weather in the straits, even though he had started from the west.

In 1525 Vice Admiral Sebastian Cano only managed to make his way back to the Pacific Ocean after three months of arduous navigating.

In 1540, only one of Alfonso de Camargo's three-vessel squadron was able to get through to the straits.

On August 20 of the same year, Sir Francis Drake, sent by

Queen Elizabeth of England to destroy the Spanish colonies, penetrated the straits and emerged on December 6, after a lucky crossing.

Meanwhile, the Peruvian Pedro Sarmiento, sent with two ships from the port of Callao in Peru to combat the English fleet, approached the straits from the west, and this trip resulted in the most complete—albeit exaggeration-filled—documentation of this region. Sarmiento entered via the San Isidoro Canal, took possession of the land in the name of the King of Spain, reached the second narrows, battled natives whom he incorrectly described as giants, and returned to Europe, receiving command of a fleet of twenty-three vessels and the mission of founding a colony on the edge of the straits. But after the loss of several ships, he was reduced to a command of four hundred men from an initial crew of four thousand, with only enough provisions for eight months.

After building a fort at the entry to the straits, he advanced to their center, to the spot on which Philippeville would be built, which later was given the all-too-significant name of Port Famine. During his return, Sarmiento was captured by the British and brought to England. He had left the budding colony in a deplorable state, populated by only twenty-three men and two women. These unfortunate people, dying from hunger, tried to get back to Rio de la Plata through Patagonian territory, but were never heard from again.

A sole survivor, the colonist Hernando, was recovered by Sir Thomas Cavendish (also spelled Candish) in 1587, when the Englishman was passing within sight of Philippeville, in order to get around Cape Froward and wind up in the Pacific, a fifty-two-day crossing during which he had to repel attacks from cannibals.

Four years later, Thomas Candish returned to Port Famine and this time, after two fruitless attempts to disembogue at the Southern Sea, he was pushed back by winds and currents and forced to give up his attempt to cross the straits, returning instead to Europe.

John Childley's expedition in 1590 was equally stricken. After a call at Port Famine, it made nearly ten useless attempts to get past Cape Froward. The winds forced his ships to head back for Europe, and one of them ran aground on the Normandy shore.

In 1593, Richard Hawkins was luckier: after having discovered the Falkland Islands, he headed west, entering the straits on January 10, 1594, and arrived in sight of Cape Froward, where he was unable to debark, and finally reached the Pacific Ocean.

Then it was the turn of the Dutch, who had not reappeared in these waters since the discovery of Cape Horn.

In order to pillage the Spanish territories, Simon de Cordes left Amsterdam on June 27, 1598, with five vessels under his command. He managed to enter the straits on April 6 of the following year and put in until August 23 at the bay which was given his name. His stay on the coast was marked by devastating hardships and battles with savages, in which around one hundred Dutchmen were killed. Finally, after having emerged from the east of the straits on September 3, after having risked death in the neighboring archipelagos, he had to return, and left for Europe, arriving in January 1600.

Then came Oliver de Noort who, after five perilous attempts, dropped anchor at Cape Foreland and Port Famine, whose ruins were no longer visible, and, after putting in at Maurice Bay, had the good luck to cross the straits.

Then there was George Spilberg, who had the most fortunate of all these expeditions. Sailing on May 16, 1614 with six ships, he arrived at the straits on May 25, reached Port Famine, dropped anchor at Cordes Bay, and by May [26] was sailing on the waters of the Pacific Ocean.

Two years later, Le Maire and Schouten discovered another route from the south, passing between Tierra del Fuego and Ile des Etats, at the farthest reach of Magellania, and this channel was named the straits of Le Maire.

Garcia de Nodales was sent by the King of Spain on a mission to lay claim to the aforementioned Straits, having carefully explored them in 1618. He discovered the islands that make up today's Cape Horn Archipelago, returned west as far as the Pacific Ocean, headed for the Straits of Magellan which he entered without problem, and returned to Seville on July 9, 1619, thereby completing a marvelous expedition without losing a single crew member.

In 1669, John Narborough visited Elizabeth Island, Freshwater Bay, and Port Famine, pushing ahead as far as the Saint Jerome Canal, emerging from the straits and advancing as far as Valdivia, then returning to go back to Europe, after two years' navigation that permitted him to map these waters.

Certainly pillaging the Spanish colonies in South America was fashionable at the time. Therefore it is not surprising that the French did not delay either, like other European countries. On June 3, 1695, Captain de Gennes left La Rochelle with six ships, went round the Cape des Vierges on June 3, 1695, put in at Boucault Bay and at Saint George Island, then dropped anchor at Port Famine and Saint Nicholas Bay, which he renamed French Bay, and tried in vain to sail farther, but was obliged to return to Europe in April 1697.

In 1698, Beauchesne-Gouin followed his countryman's footsteps, but six months later only managed to get around Cape des Vierges with one of his four ships. He put in at Port Galant, and despite constant opposition of wind and current, tenaciously managed to get back to the waters of the Pacific Ocean.

Sixty years later, on June 21, 1764, Commodore Byron brought the *Dolphin* and the *Tamar* to the Cape des Vierges, made friendly contacts with the Patagonians, dropped anchor at Port Famine, and returned eastward to visit the Falklands, before reappearing in the straits on February 18, at Port Famine on the twenty-first, and getting back to the Atlantic Ocean on April 9, 1765.

At the same time, Bougainville, a French captain, commanding *L'Aigle,* reached the Cape des Vierges on February 16, 1765, went around the Cape, and put in on the twenty-first in a little bay that was named after him, and having taken on a cargo of building wood, returned in March to his colony, the Malvinas.

The following year, Captains Duclos-Guyot and La Giraudais arrived at Port Famine with the ships *L'Aigle* and *L'Etoile,* with which they pushed back an attack by the natives from this part of Brunswick Island, while signing a treaty of alliance with the Patagonians of Cape Gregory.

After Bougainville ceded his colony to the Spanish, following orders received in 1767, he wanted to make his way back to the Southern Seas by crossing the Straits of Magellan. On December fifth of that year, he entered the straits, docked at Cape Possession, had praiseworthy contact with the Patagonians, reached Port Famine on the sixteenth, and Bougainville Bay on the eighteenth, stayed twenty-six days at Port Galant, and helped by favorable winds, emerged from the straits on January 26, 1766.

Finally, Samuel Wallis, a British captain, left Plymouth on June 22, 1766, with three ships: a vessel, a store ship, and a sloop. He entered the straits on November 16, did business with the Patagonians, went to Port Famine to stock up on water and wood, and risked extreme danger with audacious bravery to arrive at the Pacific Ocean during the night of April tenth and eleventh.

Then the famous Straits were forsaken until 1826, when Captain King [Verne erroneously writes that it was Captain Wallis—Editor's note] was ordered by the British government to measure the hydrography of these Magellanic waters, a highly successful exercise supervised by Captain Fitzroy in 1834.

After this study came a new and exact scientific exploration of the straits' eastern portion between Cape des Vierges and Port Galant. Captain Dumont d'Urville brought this survey to a successful conclusion with the corvettes *The Astrolabe* and *The Zélée* during the years 1837, 1838, 1839, and 1840.

Some details of interest will follow about this memorable voyage, so honorable for France.

Orders from the Naval Minister dated August 26, 1837, stated that a new expedition would be undertaken, in order to complete the vast amount of information already gathered—both by Captain Dumont d'Urville and other seafarers of the still imperfectly described waters of the Southern Sea—to learn their hydrography, commerce, and science more precisely.

On September 7, 1837, *The Astrolabe* and *The Zélée* left Toulon for Tenerife, putting in at this island from September thirtieth to October twelfth, then crossed the Atlantic for Rio de Janeiro, set sail again on November 14, arriving at Cape des Vierges on the morning of December twelfth, and the same day, after having passed near Dungeness Point, and backed by a cool northern breeze, attained the brink of the first narrows.

From there, the corvettes entered Saint Philip's Bay, where they almost sank in the rising waves. That night, campfires alerted them to the presence of Patagonians in the northern lands, and the Pecherais to the south. During the next fifteen days, they sighted Cape Negro, Elizabeth Island, Santa Magdalena Island, and Capes Mammoth, Valentyn, and Isidore before calling at Port Famine.

Dumont d'Urville put into port at this spot from December sixteenth to twenty-eighth. The location of the Sarmiento colony was studied with great care. An excellent watering place for ships was observed, along with the fact that the Sedger River provided potable water. There were productive trips to the surrounding areas, in the forests where the expedition's botanists found the Antarctic copper beech, winter's bark, and the common barberry. Everywhere, magnificent vegetation proved that the Peruvian seafarer's choice had been most fortunate, even though nothing remained of his camp apart from its ominous name. Hydrography was also pursued. The officers collected many observations about hour angles, meteorology, physics, and tidal movements. Hunting provided abundant snipe, thrushes, geese, ducks, and other aquatic animals—and fishing garnered sand gobies, grey mullets, sparlings, lampreys, abundant mussels, limpets, murexes, sea unicorns, and fissurellas. They even found a so-called "post-office," a barrel hanging from a tree branch that contained notes about a previous expedition. Dumont d'Urville had placed a marker at the top of Santa Anna Peninsula, with a pillar box lined with zinc, guaranteed to remain intact for a long time.

The commander and his officers had wanted to enter into communication with the Patagonian natives, at this time still creatures of legend. But even though trips for this purpose were made to the south of Port Famine, where ruins of ajoupas, horse carcasses, and other debris were often seen, it proved impossible to make contact with these supposed giants of the human race.

The Astrolabe and *The Zélée* set sail again on December 28, after the commander deposited his report in the "post office" he had constructed. The corvettes followed each other past Eagle, Geese Indian, Dubouchage, Bournand, Bougainville, and Nicolas Bays, admiring the wooded coastline, terraced in tiers, which joined it to the white peaks of Mounts Tarn and Nodales, and the Cape Froward mountain range. To the south, the Fuegian coastline looked more jagged, with oddly shaped rocks, and an orographic system in which pyramids, domes, and deep indentations appeared, over dark ravines. But the sparse vegetation grew increasingly scarcer as the ships went around Cape Froward.

On the twenty-ninth, Captain d'Urville reached Fortescue Bay, an excellent place to drop anchor at the entrance to Port Galant. At this time, the temperature was unusually high for these waters, which were located at a high latitude, and the thermometer measured no less than 14 degrees centigrade [57.2 degrees Fahrenheit] in the shade.

Port Galant would remain the farthest point reached during this exploration of the Straits of Magellan, about halfway along. A precise map was drawn. The place was very picturesque, a basin framed by beautiful mountains with snowy peaks.

The commander abandoned his project to reach the Pacific Ocean from the west, because he found it was too late in the season, and also because he wanted to meet the Patagonians. On December 31, the corvettes left Port Galant and headed for the opposite coast. Once Cape Froward had been passed, they took on water at the Gennes River; the officers went on new and productive expeditions, with plant-gathering and hunting, to the vicinity of Saint Nicolas Bay, which Bougainville had called French Bay.

On January 2, 1838, *The Astrolabe* and *The Zélée* raised anchor and sailed toward Nassau Island, then toward Cape Isidore. When Dumont d'Urville had arrived at Port Famine, near Point Anna, he sent a dinghy to deposit a second report in the "post office" chest. He hoved to all night, and starting on the morning of January third, went by calm seas and a favorable southern breeze, alongside Tierra del Fuego, with its low coast scattered with large rocks. But just as there were no Patagonians to be seen on the Brunswick Peninsula, so no Pecherais appeared on the Fuegian land, only a few guanacos and thousands of cormorants.

After having verified the position in longitude from Port Famine, as marked in King's maps, Commander Dumont d'Urville noticed a Patagonian campground as he sailed close to the mainland, whose tents occupied shoreline, with an American flag waving over them. It was the long-awaited occasion to enter into communication with them. Therefore the corvettes dropped anchor in Peckett Harbor, scraping their keels somewhat.

All officers were given the authorization to go ashore where the Patagonians welcomed them with a great show of friendship. *The Astrolabe's* dinghy brought aboard three of these natives, who were between 1.72 and 1.76 meters tall [between 5 feet 6 inches and 5 feet 8 inches]. They were well proportioned, with olive skin, long black hair, low receding foreheads, eyes close together, prominent cheekbones, without beard or body hair. They had lazy demeanors and were decently garbed in the national costume made of guanaco skins. Among these Patagonians were a Swiss man and an Englishman, who, having tired of this existence, obtained permission to board the corvettes.

A few days after having met the Patagonians, the officers were able to observe the Pecherais, who evidently belonged to the same race, but were more sickly and impoverished, and whose childhood was often spent in servitude.

On January 8 the expedition was completed, and after twenty-seven days spent visiting the Straits of Magellan, *The Astrolabe* and *The Zélée* returned to the waters of the Atlantic, ready to continue their adventurous trip to the mysterious region of circumpolar waters.

Such was the start of *The Astrolabe* and *The Zélée's* trip to the South Pole, under the command of ship's captain Dumont d'Urville. The straits between Patagonia and Tierra del Fuego and Dawson, Clarence, and Desolation Islands had a 560-kilometer expanse, and he thereby saved a trip of [. . .] miles. French seafarers had just traveled through two-thirds of its expanse, having drawn around ten maps of bays and ports, as the trip's log recounts, and collecting a mass of documents and materials of every kind containing great scientific interest. In general, they had good luck with climacteric conditions, except when raging squalls greeted them at Peckett Harbor. We must not forget that the two corvettes were only sailing vessels, and because of prevailing western winds that dominate, the straits are easily navigable from west to east; sailing is difficult for ships trying to go from the Atlantic to the Pacific.

True, in our day, steamers equipped with powerful engines conquer these difficulties more easily, and the passage takes place under infinitely more advantageous conditions. Plus, the straits contain an auspiciously located port of call, which is guaranteed a fine future in maritime and business affairs. This is not at the ancient port at Sarmiento, whose ruins were never found, even though it did possess excellent places for anchoring. It is rather Punta Arenas, located a little farther north on the same coastline as the Brunswick Peninsula, a colony that is newly enlarged each year.

Bringing to light the geographical arrangement of the Straits of Magellan helps give this story a solid basis. All of its southern portion belongs to Magellania, and the American continent is rounded off between the two oceans by an archipelago of islands and islets. The events involved in this story attracted the attention of the scientific and business worlds. As for Cape Horn, the partner of the Cape of Good Hope at the edge of Africa, it should be more aptly renamed Cape Tempest.

IV

MYSTERIOUS EXISTENCE

Tierra del Fuego makes up the largest part of the Magellanic domain. It is bounded on the north and west by jagged coastline, with the projections of Capes Orange, Catherine, Number, and San Diego, with Saint Sebastian and Aguirre Bays from Espiritu-Santo promontory up to Magdalena Sound. After the frayed peninsula overlooked by Mount Sarmiento projected to the west, it continued to the southeast to San Diego point—a sort of crouching sphinx, whose tail dips into the waters of the Le Maire Straits.

Along the southern coastline appears Beagle Canal, bordered on its opposite bank by Gordon, Hoste, Navarin, and Picton Islands. The changeable Cape Horn Archipelago is scattered farther to the south.

The longboat had just gone down Beagle Canal from the east, bringing the Indian's body to the Wallah campground. After leaving the Fuegian families who lived on this part of the coast, Kaw-djer and his companion headed toward one of the islands located at the straits' entrance. There the mysterious character lived, in solitary retreat, almost beyond the populated world.

It seemed as if Kaw-djer only had contact with these Tierra del Fuego natives, called Pecherais because their livelihood came from fishing [*Pêcher* meaning "to fish" in French]. Indeed, he was never seen traveling to the portion of the American continent covered by the Patagonian territories, nor did he go farther north to

Argentinean possessions, or west to the Chilean republic's provinces. The *Wel-kiej* only sailed between the banks of the Magellan Straits, and never put in to port anywhere on the Brunswick Peninsula.

At this time, Argentina on the one side and Chile on the other laid claim to Patagonia, but the line between the two republics was not yet drawn; these claims were limited to the edge of the straits, and all Magellania could be seen as an independent domain, where various tribes of Yacana Indians lived, whether migratory or settled. It was a supremely free land, a mostly deserted area not even claimed by its own natives, which no power had grabbed, not even England, its neighbor in the Falkland Islands.

Was this the determining reason that the stranger chose this faraway country to settle in? What reason—most likely a serious one—made him leave his homeland, voluntarily or not? None of the barely civilized beings with whom he was now reduced to living—the Fuegians who shared his life—thought to ask him about it. Anyway, it seems unlikely that any question would have been answered.

Five or six years earlier, the man whom the Indians would later call Kaw-djer was first seen on the coast of Tierra del Fuego. How had he arrived there? No doubt aboard one of those British ships that do coastal trading between the Falklands and the Magellanian islands. There was frequent, if not regular, maritime service between the two, sailboats or steamers that traded with the foreigners at various points of the vast archipelago. Moreover, this trade was not limited to the Magellanic domain. It extended past the Pacific Ocean, to the larger islands: Hanover, Wellington, and Chiloé, as well as the Chonos Archipelago, neighboring the Chilean republic, where British, French, and German colonies had been founded. What's more, there existed a major trade with the Fuegians for the skins of guanacos, vicunas, nandus, and sea lions. Finally whaling—whether in Magellanic waters or along the latitudes of the Polar Sea—attracted a certain number of ships, accustomed to the roundabouts of this maritime labyrinth.

The stranger's arrival could certainly be explained this way, and as stated above, it happened five or six years earlier, when he began his itinerant life among the Yacana tribes and other Fuegians.

As for the other questions, who was this man? What was his nationality? Did he belong by birth to the Old or New World? These questions about him were still open.

Everything about him was unknown, not just his status and origins, but even his name. In the free territories of independent Magellania, where no higher authority governed, who could have interrogated him about these matters? It was not like one of the states of America or Europe, where the police are concerned with people's pasts, and it is impossible to remain unknown for long. Here no official representative of any government lived, neither on the large Fuegian island nor in the archipelago nearby, and the administrative power of Punta Arenas' governor did not yet reach past the Straits of Magellan. Therefore no one could force the stranger to reveal his identity. Rare are the countries where one may live outside of all customs and laws, in the most complete independence, without being troubled by any social ties, and someday they may be totally extinct.

For the first two years after his arrival at Tierra del Fuego, Kaw-djer did not seek a home in one place rather than another. He was in constant contact only with natives, and never approached the foreign trading posts set up here and there by colonists, no matter what their nationality. He went from tribe to tribe, from campground to campground, and he was welcomed everywhere because they knew him to be helpful and kind. He lived as these natives did, from hunting and fishing, sometimes among the seaside families, and other times among the small tribes in the interior, sharing their ajoupas, wigwams, and tents. Vigorous, blessed with ironclad health and extraordinary endurance, he might have accomplished great things had he been possessed by a passion for discovery akin to Livingstone, Stanley, and Nansen. But then he would have required another setting than the Magellanic domain, whether nothing remained to be discovered after the work of Fitzroy and King.

No doubt, Kaw-djer was highly educated, mainly in the experimental sciences. He must have studied medicine quite thoroughly, as he was both a doctor and a naturalist with a far-reaching knowledge of plants' classifications and properties. He also spoke several languages fluently, so that if he had had contact with British, French, German, Norwegian, or Spanish traders, any of them might have taken him for a fellow countryman. But, after a few questions initially posed about his nationality, which he dodged, there was never any further attempt to penetrate his anonymity.

We should add that this enigmatic character quickly learned the Yaghon language. He fluently spoke this idiom, which is the most popular Magellania, into which the missionaries translated a few passages of the Bible. He only entered into contact with the ships that put into port at some spots along the Magellan Straits, the Beagle Canal, or other sounds of the Cape Horn Archipelago, in order to replenish his munitions and pharmaceutical items. He paid for these purchases by trading, or with Spanish and British money, of which he seemed to have a supply. However, had it been strictly necessary, his highly skilled hunting and fishing could have sufficed for his needs.

If a disgust for humanity, or irresistible misanthropy, had moved him to flee his fellow man and hide in this land at the back of the beyond, why did he show such kindness, generosity, and devotion to the Magellanian natives? From his sober and dejected face, one could deduce that life had disappointed him—perhaps some ambitious dreams that didn't come true, including perhaps the dream of reforming a social system that he found unacceptable. And who knows if this misanthropy was not paired with a broader hatred for mankind, apart from the poor Fuegian Indians?

During the first part of his stay, for around eighteen months, Kaw-djer never left the large island on which he had debarked.

He quickly won the natives' confidence, and his influence over their tribes grew accordingly. They came from other islands, like Hoste, Navarin, and Wollaston, to consult him. These various islands are inhabited by the Canoes or Indians with pirogues—slightly different from the Yacana race—who lived from hunting and fishing like their congeneric neighbors. They traveled to see their benefactor whenever he was in any campground on the coastline of Beagle Canal. Kaw-djer never refused advice or medical care to anyone. Often, in emergencies, when an epidemic attacked one or another of the settlements grouped around the missionaries, he would rush in to fight the disease, while still maintaining an extreme reserve about himself. Soon his fame spread through the entire region. It went farther than the Straits of Magellan. It was known that a foreigner who lived on Tierra del Fuego had received the title of Kaw-djer from the grateful Pecherais. But when he was asked on numerous occasions to go to Punta Arenas, that is to enter into contact with the Chilean township, he always refused, no matter what the circumstance. It seemed he did not wish to go anywhere that he did not consider free land.

Then, after eighteen months, an incident occurred that would change the foreigner's way of life.

Although Kaw-djer insisted on not going to Brunswick Island, which was part of Patagonian territory, the Patagonians sometimes invaded the Fuegian territory. Their small crafts brought them to the opposite banks of the Straits of Magellan in just a few hours.

Not only did they come in person, but also with campground equipment. They made lengthy trips on horseback to the interior, what Americans call big "raids," from one end of Tierra del Fuego to the other.

Thus the tireless horsemen presented themselves after having covered the vast mountainous region that made up the island's northern orographic relief—sometimes around Cape Orange at the opening of the second narrows, and sometimes at Cape Espiritu-

Santo at the very opening of the straits. They were also seen on the Atlantic coast, going from bay to bay, robbing Fuegians, attacking them if they resisted, then robbing them, plundering what they had hunted and fished, and kidnapping children, whom they brought to Patagonian tribes and held in slavery until adulthood. They sometimes launched a spearhead as far as Cape San Diego, or Le Maire Straits, against which some of the last contours of Fuegian land were outlined. On several occasions, Kaw-djer met them when they returned through Beagle Canal, heading toward the peninsula that was strangely scored by outbranchings from Mount Darwin and Mount Sarmiento. He avoided them, fleeing and warning the Indians to beware after recognizing their tracks on a campground's outskirts. Until then, he had never had contact with these savage pillagers whom Chile and Argentina could not control.

Between the Patagonians and Fuegians, there were fairly considerable ethnic differences, in terms of ancestry as well as customs—the former were infinitely more dangerous than the latter.

The Patagonians are Tehuelhets, and the Fuegians are Yacanas. The original habitat for both was Patagonia, namely that extent of territory included between Chile, Argentina, and the Atlantic Ocean. But the strong triumphed over the weak, and the Fuegians, pushed back and pursued, had to leave the continent and take refuge in the islands.

The Patagonians must have diminished in the public's opinion—in terms of their height, since it became necessary to forsake the legends of Sarminento and other seafarers. Measuring an average of 1.73 meters tall [about 5 feet 7 inches], and well proportioned, they had olive skin and black hair held in place on the forehead by a headband, which fell in back on their wide shoulders, and they had neither beard nor body hair. Their faces were wider at the jaw than at the temples, and their eyes were slightly elongated, as per the Mongol type. Their noses were flat, and their eyes shone at the back of rather narrow sockets.

Some Pecherais families may still be found on the American continent, on the other side of the Magellan Straits, but only on the coastline, and maybe in the western part where forests and mountains are found. The center, with plains as far as the eye can see, and interminable prairies, is Patagonian territory par excellence. Fearless and tireless horsemen, they needed wide spaces to cover with their no less tireless mounts, immense pasturelands to feed their horses, and hunting grounds where they went after guanacos, vicunas, and ostriches.

There is one more difference worth noting between these two Indian races.

While the Patagonians form compact tribes under a chief's authority, like the proud Kongre, and the Cacique mentioned by Dumont d'Urville, the Pecherais almost entirely lack social organization, and gather according to family in the same campground. They are fishermen rather than hunters. They spend most of their lives aboard their canoes rather than on horseback, going through Magellania's many winding curves.

The Fuegians are slightly shorter than the Patagonians. They are recognizable by their large square heads, faces with prominent cheekbones, sparse eyebrows, and more noticeably sloping skulls. They are seen as fairly miserable beings, whose race is nevertheless not extinct, for they have many children, one might say as many as the dogs that swarm around their campgrounds.

It is certain that even in our day, as in the time when *The Astrolabe* and *The Zélée* made their trips, the Pecherais suffer a great deal from their neighbors the Patagonians. The latter frequently invaded Tierra del Fuego, as we have said, and pursued the unfortunate Yacanas, who were unable to defend themselves, and kidnapped young children, whom they made into slaves until they were eighteen or twenty years old.

In November 1874, Kaw-djer intervened in an attack against the Pecherais from Useless Bay, when his wanderings led him to the western coast of Tierra del Fuego, along the Magellan Straits.

Useless Bay, bordered to the north by swampland, makes a deep indentation almost in front of the site where Sarmiento established the Port Famine colony.

Some of the Tehuelhets, after having debarked with their canoes on the southern bank of Useless Bay, threw themselves upon a Yacana campground, which contained only about twenty families. The assailants had the advantage of numerical superiority, for they were around one hundred men, stronger and better armed than the natives, who were unable to repel the attack.

However, they courageously tried to resist, thanks to the presence of a Canoe Indian who had just reached the campground in his pirogue.

This man was called Karroly—the Indian mentioned earlier. He worked as a hobbling pilot, guiding the coastal trading ships that traveled between the banks of Beagle Canal and the Cape Horn Archipelago's islands.

On his return from Punta Arenas, where he had guided a Norwegian ship that entered through Darwin Sound, he put in to port in Useless Bay, before returning to Beagle Canal.

Karroly organized the counterattack and tried to push back the aggressors, helped by the Yacanas. But the match was too uneven. The Pecherais could not offer up a serious defense. Their campground was invaded, their tents overturned, and blood was shed. Nothing could prevent the pillaging and dispersion of these families, who were obliged to flee toward the island's interior.

In Karroly's boat sat his son, Halg, a fifteen-year-old boy who helped him in his work as pilot, and who was always with him since the death of his Fuegian mother some years before.

During the battle the boy stayed aboard the pirogue, waiting for his father to rejoin him and sail off, when two Patagonians ran in his direction.

The young boy didn't want to push his canoe off the bank, which would have put him out of reach, but which would have also taken away his father's escape route.

One of the Tehuelhets leapt into the small boat, grabbing the child in his arms . . .

At this moment, Karroly ran from the campground that was now in the aggressors' hands. He saw the Tehuelhet carrying his son across the beach. He ran toward him . . . An arrow, shot by the other Patagonian, whistled by his ear, missing him . . .

At that moment, a firearm went off.

The kidnapper, mortally wounded, rolled on the ground, and the young boy ran back to his father, saved.

The other Patagonian took off by way of the campground . . .

The shot was fired by a man who had just arrived at the battle scene, Kaw-djer.

They did not pause for a moment. The pirogue's moorings were vigorously hauled. Kaw-djer, Karroly, and the boy leapt aboard, and when it was a cable's length from shore, the Patagonians covered it with a hail of arrows, one of which hit the young boy.

The campground had been entirely destroyed, and the Yacanas, many of whom had died in the attack, were dispersed throughout the countryside.

Such were the circumstances under which Kaw-djer and the Canoe Indian were brought into contact. They already knew one another, having met when the "benefactor" had visited the beach campgrounds during his endless tours through Tierra del Fuego.

The child's wound was fairly serious. Therefore Kaw-djer did not want to leave him, as long as his care was needed. The father threw himself upon his knees, repeating:

"Heal him . . . heal him!"

"I will heal him," replied Kaw-djer, once he had checked that the wound was not a mortal one.

With its sail raised, the pirogue went alongside the southern bank, and emerged at Useless Bay, with a favorable northern breeze. It went down the straits, after having gone round Cape Valentyn at the edge of Dawson Island. It arrived at Beagle Canal by way of Clarence Sound, by skirting the island with the same name, and Cockburn Canal. Forty-eight hours later, it paused in a well-shielded little creek on New Island, located at the canal's entrance.

By then the young boy was out of danger. His wound was beginning to heal. Karroly did not know how to express his gratitude to Kaw-djer, who had twice saved his child.

When the pirogue moored at the back of the creek, and the Indian debarked, he asked Kaw-djer to follow him.

"My house is here," he said. "This is where I live with my boy . . . Would you like me to show you the way? . . ."

"Yes, Karroly."

"If you want to stay here for a few days, you'll be welcome, then my pirogue will take you to the other side of the canal. If you want to stay forever, my home is your home, and I will be your companion. Here, you will be at home . . ."

"Maybe," replied Kaw-djer, profoundly touched by the affection which the Indian showed him.

At that time, the boy was only around ten years old. He was strong for his age, much toughened by his father's rough job. Ordinarily, he accompanied him aboard ships that he piloted. But after some years went by, he often stayed on New Island, and as we have seen at the beginning of this story, he was not with his father when Kaw-djer and Karroly brought back the Indian wounded by the jaguar to the Wallah campground.

From this day on, Kaw-djer remained on New Island with Karroly and his son. Their house became his permanent home. All three lived a communal life, to which some improvements and better conditions were added.

Thanks to Kaw-djer's money, the New Island home became more comfortable, among other things. But this new existence did not distract the "benefactor" from his charitable work. He made as many visits to native tribes, often with Karroly accompanying him, when they called for him.

Soon, Karroly was able to work as a pilot more profitably and with fewer dangers. Instead of his fragile pirogue, he sailed a solid longboat, the *Wel-kiej*, purchased after a Norwegian vessel was shipwrecked in the Wollaston Island channel. Karroly, an excellent sailor, had a boat that permitted him to make long crossings, and he was able to extend his piloting to the whole eastern region of the Magellan Straits.

Several years went by in this way, and it did not seem as if Kaw-djer's life, deliberately set up on independent terms in a free land, could ever be disturbed, when an unexpected and improbable event disrupted its progress.

V

NEW ISLAND

New Island is located at a forward position overlooking the entrance from the east to Beagle Canal. Two leagues in length and one league wide, it is an irregular pentagon in shape. It has plenty of trees, most particularly the Antarctic beech, as well as the winter bark, myrtle, and some medium-sized cypresses. On the prairie surface are several species of sharp-leaved shrubs, hollies, barberries, and short-growing bracken. There is good soil, or humus, appropriate for raising vegetables in certain protected places. Elsewhere, when the humus was too sparse, especially at the outskirts of the shore, nature embroidered a tapestry of lichens, moss, and lycopodium.

The Indian Karroly had lived for about ten years on this island, on the other side of a high cliff, facing the sea. He was the only inhabitant—the only settled one, at any rate—but in good weather, some Fuegians came to fish for sea perch and other amphibians usually found in these waters. They set up their tents at the back of a creek, and Karroly never had any reason to complain about their presence. At the first sign of bad weather, they disappeared, and New Island regained its usual calm.

For six years, the island had also had another inhabitant, Kawdjer, whose itinerant life finally changed after meeting Karroly. The Canoe Indian's home became his own, and he spent all his time there, when not traveling through Magellania.

As a pilot, Karroly could not have chosen a more favorable or better situated base. All the ships emerging from Le Maire Straits passed in view of New Island. If they sought to reach the Pacific Ocean by turning around Cape Horn, they had no need for a pilot. But if in order to trade along the archipelago, they wished to cross several channels, going from Deceit to Hermitte, from Freycinet to Grevy, Herschell to Wollaston, and even to Hoste, Navarin, or up the whole length of Beagle Canal, a pilot became indispensable, and they could not find a more intelligent and informed one than the Indian Karroly from New Island, who knew the sounds and channels of this labyrinth better than anyone.

In any case, few ships visited the Magellanic waters, and their business would not have earned a living for Karroly and his son. They also went hunting and fishing to obtain items for trading. Naturally, these objects, such as ruminants' skins, amphibians' pelts, and ostrich feathers, were bartered for any necessities of clothing and food, as well as rigging for the pirogue. Had he been paid in piastres for his piloting, he might have been able to spend the money at Punta Arenas, but only at this Chilean colony, for during this period no other township existed Magellania. Ushaia Colony had not yet been founded, and several years would go by before the Argentinean republic would lay its foundations on the coast of Beagle Canal.

Therefore Karroly added his skills as a hunter and fisherman to his work as pilot. Fishing was the most widely popular professional activity in the area, which included coastal trading between the islands of the archipelago.

However, although fishing was always remunerative, only after Kaw-djer moved onto New Island did hunting become productive. No doubt, this island of small dimensions could only contain a limited number of guanacos and vicunas, which are sought for their fur. On the other hand, feathered prey, including nandus, were also scarce on the beaches and interior plains. Therefore, in itself New Island did not provide a large enough hunting field. Nearby lay considerably bigger islands like Navarin, Hoste, Wollaston, and Dawson, not to mention Tierra del Fuego with its immense plains and deep forests, where ruminants and wild animals propagated.

In a few hours, the pirogue could carry Kaw-djer and Karroly from one island to another, crossing the Beagle Canal to drop them on the Fuegian banks, from which they brought the carcasses of animals killed with bullets or arrows to New Island. Later, after they bought the longboat, they could travel as far as the channels of Clarence Island and Tierra del Desolation, in the entire eastern part of the Magellan Straits. Many times, the inhabitants of Punta Arenas were visited by the *Wel-kiej*, which came either to sell furs or procure various items and stock up on munitions. But Kaw-djer was never aboard during these calls at port, and never debarked at any part of Brunswick Island whatsoever. Never had the Chilean colony's governor been honored by his visit, although he had often heard about "the benefactor" whose influence continually grew among the Fuegian tribes. His Excellency wished to get to know him and sent him an invitation to Punta Arenas; Kaw-djer did not come, refusing any contact with the Chilean colony. When the governor made inquiries, his investigations failed, and he was unable to collect any information about this mysterious character's past.

It is probable that if Magellania had been a Chilean or Argentinean possession, Kaw-djer would have been summoned to declare his nationality, and recount under what circumstances he had moved to the remote regions of Cape Horn.

Magellania's climate is much less rigorous than one may be inclined to believe. The abundant vegetation on the ground proves its mildness. Summers are hot, but winters do not bring the extreme cold felt in other lands at the same latitude, for example, the territories of North America, Canada, and British Columbia. In the winter season, the waters do not ice over, preventing longboats from sailing, at least not in Beagle Canal. Kaw-djer's trips were therefore only rarely interrupted, and unless the sea was not navigable, the Fuegian campgrounds could count on his usual visits.

Sometimes, during these absences, the young boy remained in the home on New Island. In any event, they were not long, a week at most. And sometimes Kaw-djer stayed there alone, when piloting took Karroly and his son some distance into the straits.

New Island, along with most of the islands created as a result of a violent telluric revolution that fragmented the end of the American continent, is made of sandy soil shored up by granite blocks.

The house stood at the foot of a large bluff, shielded against violent winds. For a long time, Karroly's only home was a natural cave, dug into the bluff's granite, which was considerably better than a tent, wigwam, or Yacana-style ajoupa. It looked out on the back of a little bay untroubled by the swells of the open sea, in which the pirogue had nothing to fear. This arrangement sufficed for the Indian and his son. But after Kaw-djer's arrival, a house was built slightly to the left of the cave, made up of a ground floor, with wood from the island's forests as the framework, its rocks the stonework, and lime composed of a myriad of seashells, terebratulae, surf clams, tritons, and sea unicorns.

Inside this house were three rooms, each illuminated by a window with solid shutters. In the center was a living room with a vast chimney. To the left was Kaw-djer's room, very basically furnished with bed, chairs, tables, and a few shelves. To the right was the room lived in by Karroly and his son, even more modestly furnished. On the other side, a kitchen was equipped with a cast-iron oven and furnished with various items. Workers from the Malvinas had built the house, its owner paying for them out of his pocket.

Sailing, fishing, and hunting equipment, other supplies, and firewood abundantly provided by driftwood and the island's forests were stored in a cave where treated skins and furs to be traded were also kept.

As soon as the longboat appeared in view of the island, Halg, followed by his faithful dog, Zol, barking joyously, rushed to the beach ahead of Kaw-djer and his father, who squeezed him in his arms. Then, after mooring the *Wel-kiej* at the back of the creek,

Karroly and his son carried the rigging, furs, and jaguar skins into the cave.

Kaw-djer headed for the house, went to his room and opened the shutters, letting in floods of light and air.

Everything was in order. Halg had stood watch; the young boy was trustworthy, intelligent, zealous, and they left him in charge of watching the house with confidence. In any case, no one debarked on New Island during the winter, and during the summer, the only visitors were Fuegians who came in case of emergency.

Kaw-djer seemed to go to his room with a certain satisfaction. There he found his papers and books arranged on a shelf, mostly works on medicine and political or societal economics. A cupboard held various vials and surgical instruments. There Kaw-djer placed the medical kit that he took out of his game bag and put his gun in the corner. Then, seated at the table, he took out his notebook and recorded the incidents which had marked this latest trip on Fuegian land, according to their date.

Once that was accomplished, after a change of clothes, he came out of the house, just as Karroly and Halg were finishing their work.

The young boy left them and went to the kitchen where he lit the oven while waiting for his father's return.

After reuniting, Kaw-djer and Karroly approached an enclosure from the left, located at the foot of the bluff. The wooden fence around it protected it against infestation by rodents, which were numerous on the island.

There, over a surface of two or three acres were squares of rich soil, used for growing vegetables—cabbage, potatoes, and especially celery, the antiscorbutic properties of which are much appreciated in high latitudes—Perdicium lettuces, and also azorella, a plant with yellow leaves that resembles the Malvinas gum tree. The azorella's roots have a rather pleasant sugary taste. Although they are actually not very nourishing, the natives make bread out of them.

Some trees, among them the loranthus, decorated this enclosure with scarlet flowers, while here and there different plants were grouped, including the maritime aster, in subtle shades of blue and purple, yellowish leopard's bane, slipperwort, and laburnum creeping on the ground.

The enclosure was in good condition, like the house, thanks to Halg's care. In any case, the others had only been absent about two weeks. Apart from unforeseen circumstances, Kaw-djer never left New Island any more, except for hunting and fishing expeditions. The month of May began, which corresponded to the month of November in the northern hemisphere. Winter would quickly wrap Magellania in its snows and hoarfrost. There was plenty of work to do, for the most fruitful season for fishing approached, or rather, for hunting sea lions.

When Kaw-djer and Karroly finished their visit, they headed for the cave. That's where their warehouse of merchandise was kept. Inside this vast excavation, carpeted with fine sand, with walls of dry materials that humidity never penetrated, were piled skins of cougars, jaguars, guanacos, vicunas, and nandus.

These pelts, treated according to the Patagonian method, were much softened, especially the guanacos, and in this guise, could serve as outer garments. The chiefs wore such garments when they dressed in national costume. At the same time, rugs were made of them, as sought after as the rugs made of ostrich skin. These items made by Fuegian workers were the basis for major trading with traffickers.

But most of all, the cave contained a stock of sea lion skins. The hunt for these amphibians, which are so numerous in the archipelago channels, should reap substantial rewards for Magellania, when the fishing grounds become subject to indispensable regulation. This hunting is very difficult and even quite dangerous, as the sea lion favors sheer coastal cliffs and the most inaccessible crests, and one must block his path to the sea where he can outrace any pursuer. Thus sea lion hunters need strength as well as dexterity, and risk frightening falls. But their efforts are well compensated. Unfortunately, the hunters are the worst kind of adventurers, with no respect for laws or belief, who care nothing for social conventions, and generally are no better than gold prospectors. And they hang about the Magellanic waters for long periods, for when the gold-bearing deposits of these regions are exhausted, thousands of sea lions will still furnish ships with opulent cargos.

Such was the arrangement at New Island since Kaw-djer moved in to live with Karroly and his son. They lacked nothing. The guanaco would have sufficed for nourishing food. Its meat, so tasty when grilled, is also fine when cut into pieces, tenderized between two stones, hung up to age, then cured, left in the open air for a few weeks, and finally served in potted form.

In addition, the island's bays swarmed with fish like grey mullets, sparlings, and loaches. The seashore contained abundant edible mollusks, among them inexhaustible beds of mussels. Aquatic prey pullulated along the coastline.

The sweet-water source was a river descending from the southwest, more a torrent than a stream, which no pirogue could have climbed against the current. Its own source was a hill slope 250 feet high, sheltered by large copper beeches, which dropped down into the sea to the left of the hillock. The river's narrow, deep mouth squeezed between two peaks, provided an excellent moorage for the longboat.

As winter approached, life as usual resumed at this New Island home. Some Falkland Island coasting vessels visited to pick up pelts before snowstorms made the waters unnavigable. The skins were sold at a good price or traded for provisions and munitions, which were necessary during the harsh weather from June to September, when the temperature was almost never higher than about ten degrees above zero, centigrade [around 50 degrees Fahrenheit].

During the last week of May, Kaw-djer remained alone with the young boy on New Island. Karroly had been hired for a piloting job and embarked aboard a Danish schooner which, to avoid the stormy waters around Cape Horn, went from the Atlantic

Ocean to the Pacific through Beagle Canal. Aided by prevailing winds, the longboat returned without problem to its little home port.

Kaw-djer felt much love for the young boy, then age seventeen, and who returned a filial respect for the man. Perhaps his affection for Karroly and his son was the only tie that linked him to humanity, after how many unknown disappointments.

Kaw-djer had worked to develop the child's intelligence, by teaching him about things he could understand. Of course, the father and son, removed from the savage state so to speak, were quite different from the Magellanian natives, who were so removed from the rest of civilization.

Of course, Kaw-djer always conveyed the ideas of independence and liberty that were dearest to him to young Halg. In him, Karroly and his son did not see a master, but an equal. He was no kind of master, just as no man worthy of the name needs a master. It is no surprise that, faithful to his sad motto, he sought to destroy in them any religious feeling, which can be found even among small tribes of the lowest order. He would no sooner admit God's existence than submit to a master's domination.

Supposedly, missionaries met several times during their evangelical trips with Kaw-djer, whose inexhaustible charity and tireless devotion to the unfortunate Pecherais surely attracted their admiration. They tried to get into contact with "the benefactor." One of them, from the Mission of [. . .] wanted to see him, and had himself brought to New Island. But faced by a man who was so peremptory in his ideas, so resistant to any discussion about religion or society, all he could do was withdraw. It was similar to what happened at the Wallah campground when Fathers Athanase and Severin came to say their last prayers over the Indian's corpse. When they thanked him, Kaw-djer merely said before leaving, "I only did my duty!"

In June, winter suddenly hit Magellania. The cold was not extreme, but the entire area was swept with blustery winds. New Island, like the rest of the archipelago's islands, was hidden by heaps of snow. Frightening storms troubled the waters, and Punta Arenas, lost in its isolation on the Brunswick Peninsula, was not visited by any more ships. No ships dared to cross the straits at this time of year.

June, July, and August went by, but in mid-September, the temperature became noticeably warmer, and the Falklands coasting vessels started to be seen in the channels.

On September 19, an American steamer appeared at the Canal's entryway, its pilot flag at the foremast. Karroly, leaving Kaw-djer behind on New Island, embarked on this steamer heading for Chonos, along the Chilean coast.

He was absent for about a week, and when the longboat brought him back, Kaw-djer asked him about various events of the trip, as usual.

"Nothing went wrong," answered Karroly. "The sea was fair in the canal, and the wind was favorable—a northeast wind."

"And it kept up the whole time?"

"The whole time."

"Where did you leave the ship?"

"At Cockburn Sound, at the tip of Clarence Island, where we met a sloop that was going up to Tierra del Fuego."

"And the open sea?"

"A strong storm on the open sea."

As we see, these questions only dealt with maritime occurrences between New Island and Clarence Island. Kaw-djer asked for no news about the Old and New Worlds from which he had removed himself, that Karroly might have heard aboard the American ship. Kaw-djer was no longer interested in anything that happened outside the Magellanic region. He did not even wish to hear echoes of news from outside. No doubt, he had resolved to be deaf to anything that could revive his memories of the past.

However, Kaw-djer continued to ask Karroly about the American ship.

"Where did it come from?"

"From Boston."

"And where was it going?"

"To the Chonos Islands."

That was all.

Then Karroly thought he had better speak some more about the sloop he had encountered in Cockburn Sound.

Leaving the ship, his longboat went toward Beagle Canal and put into port for a few hours on the southern bank of Tierra del Fuego, overlooked by Mount Sarmiento.

There, in a cove along the coast was the sloop in question, with a troop of soldiers debarking from it.

"Soldiers of what nationality?" asked Kaw-djer.

"Chileans and Argentineans."

"What were they doing?"

"They were with two officers, reconnoitering on Tierra del Fuego and the neighboring islands, after having visited the Brunswick Peninsula."

"Where did they come from?"

"From Punta Arenas, where the governor put the sloop at their disposal."

"How long were they going to put into port?"

"Until their work was done," replied Karroly.

Kaw-djer asked no more questions of the Indian. He paused pensively. What could the presence of these officers mean? What operation could they be engaged in on this part of Magellania? Was it a geographic or hydrographic expedition? What more could one want to know, after the work of Captains King and Fitzroy, followed by that of Captain Dumont d'Urville? Was it a more thorough verification of the maritime data that these officers had collected?

Kaw-djer was plunged into thought. Worry seemed to cloud his brow. Would the two officers' mission be extended to the entire Magellanic Archipelago? Would the sloop put into port as far as the waters of New Island?

In fact, what gave a slightly worrisome importance to this matter was that the expedition was sent by both the Chilean and Argentinean governments, which meant an agreement between the two countries that claimed ownership of the region—claims that were in any case unjustified. Until then, the two countries had never managed to reach an accord.

After these few exchanges with Karroly, Kaw-djer went to the farthest point of the hillock.

From there, he could see a wider expanse of sea, and he looked instinctively toward the south, in the direction of the last land where the American continent plunges into the waters of Cape Horn. Then he transcended it, his imagination taking him beyond. In his mind, he entered the Polar Circle, and was lost amid the mysterious and deserted regions of the Antarctic, which still defied exploration, even by the most fearless discoverers.

It seemed as if Karroly had something to tell him, for having finished unloading the *Wel-kiej*, he headed for the bluff. He seemed to hesitate, and Kaw-djer, still lost in thought, did not see him approach.

After several minutes, Kaw-djer descended on the shore to return to the house, where he would withdraw as usual.

Karroly came up to him.

"Kaw-djer . . .," he said.

Kaw-djer looked at him, paused, and looked at him again, questioningly.

"I have something more to tell you," the Indian declared.

"Speak, Karroly."

"When I was over there, at the officers' campground, one of them, the Chilean, asked me, "Who are you?" "A pilot," I answered. "The pilot Karroly of New Island?" "Yes!" "Ah, that's where Kaw-djer lives, the 'benefactor' who everyone talks about . . ." I didn't say anything. But the other officer joined us, and he added, "Well then, maybe we'll wind up meeting him, this man, and when we ask him who he is, he'd better answer us!"

VI

PUNTA ARENAS

On the morning of December 17, 1880, the sloop *Gracias a Díos* with a Chilean flag at its gaff, maneuvered along the west coastline of the Magellan Straits, so as to benefit from the first wave to drive it ashore into Punta Arenas port.

The sloop came from Gente Grande Bay, open on the other side of Tierra del Fuego's shore, and had managed to cross the Strait's twelve league length at this altitude in a few hours.

The *Gracias a Díos* was commanded by a naval lieutenant, with around twenty men under his orders, including engineers and stokers. In addition, thirty Argentinean and Chilean militiamen joined the disembarkation.

There were two passengers aboard the sloop, Superintendent Idiarte who represented Chile, and Superintendent Hererra for the La Plata provinces, or Argentinean republic.

These two notables had received from their respective governments the mission to establish Magellania the borders for the two countries that claimed possession of it. This question, which had dragged out for a number of years already, had not yet been resolved to any mutual satisfaction.

Moreover, it didn't seem as if the two superintendents had managed to agree during the course of their trip. As the sloop approached Punta Arenas, they exchanged hostile looks while avoiding running into one another on the poopdeck. The highly impatient Idiarte paced the port deck, while the agitated Herrera strode around the starboard deck. The lieutenant, coming and going on the bridge, paid no attention, doubtless accustomed to this activity, and concentrated on anchoring maneuvers to be done as soon as the tide permitted.

Around 10:15, the *Gracias a Díos* dropped its rear anchor near the riverbank facing the nearest houses of Punta Arenas. In truth, the berth was only middling and ships were poorly protected from the open seas. In this sense, Port Famine's location, to the south on the same bank as the straits, was more advantageous. There boats were better protected against northern and eastern winds, and there was room for expansion. Moreover, the watering place offered abundant, fine water, drawn from the Gennes River, and cargo ships debarked there easily.

Considering these advantages, the Chilean government had decided to rebuild the ruined colony, the former Ciudad Real of El Felipe. Port Famine became a village again, and a center for transportation was set up there. It would not last. After a revolution broke out in the city of Valparaiso in 1850, in which some of the colonies declared themselves in support of the old authorities, and others in support of the new ones, all fighting over Chile's presidency. In the end, Port Famine's governor was assassinated.

The government managed to suppress the rebellion, but from that day the colony began a steady decline. So when it became question of rebuilding a third time, another site was chosen, where Punta Arenas is still located today.

Moreover, Chile was determined that its fleet remain a presence on the western banks of the Magellan Straits and the port, which it hoped to control completely as the only port of call between the Atlantic and Pacific Oceans, would become all the more important as steamships replaced sailboats. The straits route became easily navigable for steamers despite the dominant western winds. Finally, it was definitively laying claim here, in opposition to the Argentinean republic's claims, at least in terms of the Brunswick Peninsula, as the natural prolongation of Patagonian territory.

When the anchoring maneuver finished, the two superintendents climbed into the sloop's canoe without saying a word to one another. Both debarked on a narrow embankment that formed a jetty. Then Messrs. Herrera and Idiarte each went on his own way past a lovely, carefully maintained road, leading to the township whose little bell tower pointed above the trees.

The township, and future city, had begun as a simple village. Its main street was lined with joined houses, with verandas that stretched from one end to the other. There were only two municipal buildings: the church, topped by a spire that emerged from the greenery and stood against the mountainous horizon, and the governor's residence, a quite comfortable house. In a few more years, Port Famine's fortunate competitor would add more monuments; its population would grow, and its business dealings would extend to American and European contacts.

The village was surrounded by campos—magnificent pasturing grounds for raising livestock, which are exported to great profit. The Chilean government was well aware of this. By making Punta Arenas a free port, it could offer traffickers better and cheaper merchandise than Buenos Aires. This is where they preferred to come and pick up their cargoes, instead of loading in the Argentine republic's ports. Without considering Punta Arenas' other facilities, this meant savings in transport and customs fees, as well as a trip of over fifteen hundred miles.

As we see, the colony's inhabitants were guaranteed a fine commercial future. By this time it was already on the road to prosperity from trading posts founded by British and Chilean companies and regular contact with the Falkland Islands, Magellania's neighbor. There was also a penitentiary in suitable condition, which the government made good use of.

For quite a long time, the Chilean and Argentinean governments laid claim to ownership of the Patagonian and Magellanian territories, which were still not divided between the two governments. This situation could never be solved and caused interminable discussions. Thus Tierra del Fuego and its various dependent archipelagos could be considered as independent.

However, if this state of affairs continued, it might give rise to major conflict. It was important that it be resolved, not just for political reasons, but in terms of business matters that affected other nations. It seemed at any rate as if the Punta Arenas colony accorded Chile a certain preponderance over the Magellanic domain.

To arrive at a definitive solution, the two republics appointed the two superintendents. There was no time to lose. Some emigrants flowed into the regions, attracted by the natural resources. And all-devouring England was not far off. From its Falkland archipelago, it might extend a hand as far as Magellania, and would be able to quickly cross the arm of the sea that separated it from the American continent. Already its coasting vessels were constantly present in the archipelago's channels. And its missionaries constantly applied their influence on the Fuegian people. It was time to do something.

Therefore superintendents Herrera and Idiarte arrived on board the *Gracias a Díos*, which the Chilean authorities put at their disposal. Two months before, they had left Punta Arenas, and conscientiously visited the vast collection of islands and islets from Cape Pilares on Tierra del Desolation at the western entrance of the straits to Vancouver Point at the end of Terre des Etats above Le Maire Canal, and finally to the very last island that Cape Horn offers up between the Atlantic and Pacific Oceans.

The sloop was commanded by an officer who knew all these passages and the depths of the waters perfectly well. First, the superintendents explored Patagonia and Tierra del Fuego in order to draw a contractual line separating the two countries. Then they visited the other large islands, Clarence, Desolation, and Dawson; then the medium-sized islands, Stewart, Londonderry, Navarin, Hoste, Gordon, and Wollaston; then the smallest, Gilbert, Hermitte, Grevy, Freycinet, Deceit, and Horn, not to mention New Island. But at the moment when they set foot on New Island, Kaw-djer, Karroly, and his son were away on one of their usual trips, so neither Mr. Herrera nor Mr. Idiarte could contact its mysterious dweller.

In short, when the sloop returned to Punta Arenas, the superintendents were unable to agree on fixing borders in Patagonia or Magellania. Each energetically defended his country's ideas, was very protective of its rights, and aggressive with the other. Numerous times during the expedition, violent discussions and unfortunate scenes occurred. On several occasions, the captain had to use his authority to prevent a tussle, but once on land, might these two obstinate defenders of their own countries wind up fighting a duel?

Would Chile and Argentina stand up for inspectors Idiarte and Herrera respectively, in a war declared over this question of Magellania, Santiago, and Buenos Aires by calling on the god of battles to decide borders? Who knows? Europe and America might even have to intervene in the fight.

Fortunately, Governor Aguire of Punta Arenas was a highly intelligent man, with an honest mind, who knew how to examine things with reason and composure. He knew the disputed territories completely, and independently of the two superintendents, he had apprised the presidents of Argentina and Chile of the situation.

Having learned about the hostile mood in which Messrs. Idiarte and Herrera returned from their mission, and wishing to prevent an explosion, he invited them to his office the day after their return.

The superintendents accepted Mr. Aguire's invitation.

The latter had some trouble keeping a straight face when he saw how the two individuals faced each other, the furious looks they exchanged showing a violent desire to devour one another, their determination to push things to extremes . . .One must not forget that these were men of Spanish origin and maybe the blood of Don Diego and Don Gomes [characters in Pierre Corneille's play *Le Cid* (1637)] flowed in their veins . . .

Mr. Aguire told them right off: "Gentlemen, I have received from the Chilean and Argentinean governments an order to finish this business of marking borders as quickly as possible. Please report on your mission's results. I know you've carried it out with zeal, and have no doubt that we'll arrive at . . ."

"There is no way of agreeing with Mr. Herrera!" Mr. Idiatre declared tartly.

"As for me," added Mr. Herrera, "I give up on any attempt to deal with Mr. Idiarte."

"Gentlemen, would you allow me to finish?" said the governor in a conciliatory tone. "What's the use of starting up discussions here that can't be resolved? One must not let what are questions of general interest degenerate into personal matters. That Mr. Herrera should be mortally angry at Mr. Idiarte, and that Mr. Idiarte should swear eternal hatred for Mr. Herrera, is a very regrettable state of affairs, and likely to delay the resolution of the pending case between Chile and the Argentinean republic."

The two superintendents did not reply, and Mr. Aguire continued in these terms:

"Therefore, gentlemen, forget yourselves for a moment, in order to discuss with equanimity, presenting reasons to back up your opinions. In my opinion, we have two matters to discuss: first, that of Patagonia, and second, that of Magellania.

"That of Patagonia?" shouted Mr. Idiarte. "But for a representative of Chile's interests, should that exist? Won't that resolve itself through force of circumstance?"

"Indeed," replied Mr. Herrera, who did not want to be left at a loss, "it will resolve itself, in favor of Argentina!"

"Gentlemen," the governor repeated, trying with great difficulty to control the discussion.

"But," Mr. Herrera interrupted violently, "isn't it enough to glance at a map to see that Patagonia is the geographical prolongation of Argentina, with the same climate and soil, with no natural limit other than those of the American continent! The government of Chile, by contrast, is a simple strip of seashore, separated from Patagonian territory by the barrier of the Andes, and Chile has no right to go past that mountain chain, from the geographic point of view!"

"Now, now!" shouted Mr. Idiarte. "What you just said, sir, is an unjustifiable claim, which goes against the law and common sense! And the governor of Punta Arenas, who is a Chilean citizen, is not qualified to accept it!"

"Gentlemen, let's forget that I am Chilean," said Mr. Aguire decisively, "and following my orders, I intend to treat both countries neutrally. I know that the Argentinean government has always considered Patagonia as an exclusive possession. But may I point out that Chile's possession of the Punta Arenas colony would destroy that claim? Also, without getting caught up in arguments that the two governments might equally use, I believe that we must designate a demarcation line on Patagonian territory that tells each party what he has the right to legitimately possess."

"In Patagonia, no concessions may be granted," stated Mr. Idiarte.

"None," added Mr. Herrera.

Both spoke with the kind of force that would not permit contradiction.

"However, the question must be resolved without delay," said the, "and it will happen without you, gentlemen, if you continue to refuse to compromise . . ."

At this unambiguous statement, the two superintendents remained silent. Decidedly, since they refused to reply, what good was it to have sent them on a two months' mission to these disputed territories?

The governor continued: "And now, as I said before, we must quickly resolve the second question before the first one, namely, the one about the division of Magellania. Both governments will continue to bear influence on the Patagonian territories, surely. But on Tierra del Fuego, like its surrounding archipelagos, the

Indians have always enjoyed complete independence, and the Fuegian land is not yet owned by either Chile or Argentina. No doubt, Britain desires this land that is a neighbor since the Falklands were made part of its colonial empire. Its ships visit the Magellanic Islands; its traffickers have set up business contacts with the Pecherais; its missionaries work with the native population, showing incredible tenacity; trading posts will soon be opened on the Magellan Straits and Beagle Canal. If we don't address this situation promptly, if the two republics do not manage to agree on their rights to these territories, if they continue in joint possession, that will be like saying that Magellania is up for grabs, and it will be grabbed, by the United Kingdom which will finally seize it. At all costs, let us prevent Great Britain from taking a foothold in South America, as it is already too much that she should own colonies in the Antilles Ocean and the dominion of North America!"

This was wisely thought out, from a purely American point of view, connected with the imperious Monroe Doctrine. A danger existed that could only be fended off by taking ownership, a proper division of Patagonia and Magellania between the two adjacent governments. But to arrive at this result required an agreement, which the superintendents seemed far from reaching.

"Mr. Governor," said Mr. Herrera, pursing his lips. "Your excellency has a very simple way of resolving the question, a very natural and logical means, which Mr. Idiarte has always refused to allow."

"Which is?" asked Mr. Aguire.

"It's to give up all the Patagonian territories to Argentina, and all the Magellanic territories to the Chilean republic."

"Will you look at that!" shouted Mr. Idiarte, his eyes fiery with rage, "Twenty thousand square kilometers to Argentina, and only [. . .] for Chile!"

"The two areas are the same!"

"Really, sir!" Mr. Idiarte replied bitterly. "Well, the teacher who instructed you in arithmetic stole your money!"

"I will not stand," replied Mr. Herrera, "this attempt to teach me to count!"

"Gentlemen," said the governor, who had to get between the two superintendents, who were ready to strike each other.

"And anyway," Mr. Idiarte continued furiously, "there is a reason why this proposal is immediately unacceptable."

"No there isn't! None!" shouted Mr. Herrera.

"It is the following, sir," declared Mr. Idiarte. "It's that if Patagonia is given to the Argentinean government, the Brunswick Peninsula to which it is attached will also belong to it. Then Chile will lose Punta Arenas, that thriving colony of two thousand inhabitants, destined for such a magnificent future, a Chilean colony, an ultimately Chilean colony . . ."

"Hmph!" said Mr. Herrera, who had no intention of giving in to this argument, despite its reasonableness, and pretended instead to have an answer for everything. "You'll keep your peninsula, and if need be we'll make an island of it by cutting off the isthmus."

"Gentlemen, gentlemen," said the governor, "I beg of you—leave things as nature made them, and leave isthmuses in their place! It's enough to have tried that business at Suez and Panama! Anyway, I feel that Mr. Herrera's proposal is unacceptable even if Chile keeps the Brunswick Peninsula! What is fair and logical, is for Chile and Argentina each to own an equal part of Patagonian and Magellanic territory, so that each side's interests may be fulfilled."

His Excellency spoke wisely, there is no doubt. Any other solution would be illegitimate and a source for future conflicts. Therefore all efforts headed toward this conclusion.

Then, Mr. Aguire tried to reconcile the irreconcilable superintendents. His efforts failed. Neither wished to cede the slightest bit of his claims. At the end of this meeting, they seemed all the more irritated with each other, and one could see that the quarrel would result in an explosion.

Certainly, the claims that the two governments made on the independent territories, consisting of Patagonia on one hand and Magellania on the other, had to have equal weight. There was no question of consulting the Tehuelhets and Pecherais in order to know if they would become Chilean or Argentinean. No, there would be no referendum on the subject. The question would belong entirely to the two republics. Would one of them cross the Río Negro, whose left bank was already Argentinian? Would the other cross the Andes, whose western side was already Chilean? And what would be the dividing line?

Unfortunately, one could scarcely rely on Messrs. Herrera and Idiarte to mark the borderline. The information that they sent to their governments did not permit them to make an informed decision. But doubtless their governments would know how to exploit surer and less agitated sources.

As for Mr. Aguire, he didn't know what to think about Kawdjer, whose influence was strong over the Fuegians, Yacanas, and others. The superintendents had not met him on either Tierra del Fuego or on any other islands of the Magellanic Archipelago. However, if New Island, where this personage lived, was given to Chile, the governor meant to be briefed on this subject, and he began an investigation to learn the exact position and identity of the mysterious "benefactor."

From the late interviews that Mr. Aguire had with each superintendent separately, nothing resulted that could facilitate a shared agreement. Under these conditions, how could an international treaty be sketched out which the two parliaments might vote on? The rapport between Messrs. Herrera and Idiarte continued to worsen. In vain did the governor try to bring the adversaries to a compromise. Their anger only increased. Soon a duel took place, in which Mr. Idiarte took a bullet in the right side, and Mr. Herrera a bullet in the left shoulder. It was easier to extract these bullets than to extract words of reconciliation from these two fierce enemies.

The duel did not advance the question, which would be settled at Santiago and Buenos Aires. It was a burning question, in any case. A few ominous attempts had been made by the United Kingdom, whose colors traveled more resolutely than ever across Magellania's canals and sounds. It was feared that on a given day, they might be planted somewhere, and as is well known, nothing is harder to uproot than the British colors!

Finally, on January 17, 1881, the treaty was signed in Buenos Aires by superintendents, neither of whom was Mr. Herrera or Mr. Idiarte, which permitted them to bring the matter to a conclusion.

Henceforth, it was known that a line of demarcation existed between Chile and Argentina on Patagonian territory. This line followed the Andes mountainside itself, between the banks of the Pacific and the banks of the Atlantic, ending at the fifty-second degree of latitude.

Here is what was definitively accepted by the two governments:

Starting with the fifty-second degree, a line would be extended to the east along this parallel, crossing the seventieth meridian, (72 degrees, 20' 21" to the west of the meridian of Paris). From this point, a natural line would take the crest line of the Patagonian hills along the Magellan Straits, up to Dungeness Point on Cape des Vierges.

Thus were Patagonia and Magellania divided.

Across the Tierra del Fuego territory, the borderline resumed at the level of Cape Espiritu-Santo, descending along the sixty-eighth meridian (70 degrees, 34' 21" to the west of Paris) up to Beagle Canal.

With this demarcation established, all the territories to the west belonged to Chile, and all those to the east were Argentina's.

As for the archipelago located to the south of the canal, whose farthest islet reached Cape Horn, it would be entirely Chilean, apart from Ile des Etats that the Le Maire Straits separated from the eastern limits of Tierra del Fuego, which was kept under Argentinean rule.

There was no debate over the Magellan Straits. They would remain, in absolute neutrality, open to ships from the New World and the Old.

Such was the treaty adopted and approved by both parliaments and signed by the presidents of the two American republics.

But if it ended the joint possession and established the rights of both countries, both Patagonia and Magellania lost their independence as a result. What would become of Kaw-djer on his little New Island, where his feet no longer stood on free soil, but rather Chilean territory?

VII

CAPE HORN

On January 29, the inhabitants of New Island learned of the new treaty.

Fifteen days earlier, a Russian liner, headed for Punta Arenas, appeared at the opening of Beagle Canal, requesting a pilot. The vessel took this route to the Chilean colony because it encountered violent contrary winds at the entrance to the Magellan Straits, between the Cape des Vierges and Cape Espiritu Santo. Pushed back by the currents, they descended to the Le Maire Straits, above which lay the shelter of Tierra del Fuego. Karroly went aboard at the level of New Island. Then, after an easy crossing, he returned, bringing the news that the two governments had agreed to a plan, which meant that all the islands to the south of Beagle Canal now belonged to the Chilean government.

When Karroly informed him of this unexpected news, Kaw-djer could not suppress an angry gesture. His eyes filled with hatred, and with a frightening, threatening motion, his hand stretched out toward the north. He didn't say a word, but was unable to master his excitement and took a few steps at random. It was as if the ground had given way under his feet, no longer offering him any point of support . . .

Karroly and his son did not try to intervene.

Finally, Kaw-djer managed to regain his self-control. His face, contorted for a moment, regained its usual calm and cool. Rejoining Karroly and crossing his arms over his chest, he asked in a steady tone:

"The news is definite?"

"It is," replied the Indian. "I learned it at Punta Arenas aboard a whaler that was coming in . . . Two flags have been hoisted at the entrance to the straits on Tierra del Fuego, a Chilean one at Cape Orange and an Argentinean one at Cape Espiritu-Santo.

"And," asked Kaw-djer, "all the islands to the south of Beagle Canal belong to Chile?"

"All of them."

"Even New Island?"

"Even that!"

"It had to happen!" murmured Kaw-djer, whose voice was dramatically altered with strong emotion.

He returned to the house and shut himself up in his room.

Here, and more peremptorily than ever, the question arose: who was this man? What nationality did he originally have? What reasons—no doubt very serious ones—forced him to leave one continent or another to bury his life in the solitude of Magellania? Why did he limit human contacts to a few Fuegian tribes, the unfortunate Pecherais on whom he dedicated all his intelligence and devotion?

Now that Magellania was deprived of its independence, and made up an integral part of the Chilean republic, why had this purely geographic fact so violently upset Kaw-djer? Why did the soil of New Island burn his feet?

"It had to happen!" Those were the last words he spoke.

Certainly, the treaty of January 17, 1881, would change Kaw-djer's situation, perhaps gravely so. His attitude on hearing the news from Karroly said as much, only too clearly. Motivated by highly justifiable fears, would he abandon New Island and even the Magellanic waters, which no longer offered him total security, or if he did not leave this island where he had previously hoped to spend his life without having to explain himself, would his hidden identity be brought to light?

That's what the future still concealed about the dweller on New Island. Doubtless, this would only partly satisfy the curiosity inspired by the modus vivendi of a man who only wanted to live on the margins of humanity, so to speak, and who sought refuge in the last limits of the habitable world. One must be resigned to knowing nothing about his name, identity, and origins, since the events that will occur won't force him to reveal them. But in terms of his guiding ideas, a corner of the veil covering his life can be lifted.

Kaw-djer belonged to the social category of stubborn anarchists who pushed their doctrines to extreme consequences. Having seriously studied both political and natural science, a man of courage and action resolved to make his subversive theories a reality, he wasn't the first scholar to fall into the pit of socialism, and the names of other such fearsome reformers remain in all our memories.

Socialism has been correctly defined as "that doctrine of men whose aim is no less than to change the current state of society, to reform it from top to bottom using a plan whose novelty neither excludes nor apologizes for violence."

Such was the goal which Kaw-djer foresaw, which he sought to attain *"per fas et nefas"* [Latin for "justly or unjustly"] even if it meant spending all his money and sacrificing his life to assure the final victory of his ideas.

As we know, some socialists' theories have left an indelible imprint on the history of their time.

Saint-Simon sought the abolition of privilege by birth, the suppression of inheritance, and that each person, according to his abilities, should be remunerated for his work.

Fourier preached a system of associations in his books, in which all skills would be used for the general good.

Proudhon, following a famous expression, boldly denied property rights, imagining a social order based on mutuality, in which everyone adopted the principles of an extreme individualism, in which the only condition anyone ever set was what added to his own benefit.

Other, more modern ideologists have revived these ideas of collectivity, using them as a basis for the socialization of means of production, the destruction of capital, the abolition of competition, and substitution of collective property for individual property. None of them takes into account life's contingencies; their doctrine calls for immediate and violent application; they demand mass expropriations and impose worldwide communism. Such is the banner of Lassalle and Karl Marx that is brandished and flourished, not only by Germans. Or that of Guesde, the anarchist communist leader who asks for mass expropriations. And the dangerous dreamers deploy him in front of unsettled crowds, in the name of a motto that sums it all up: expropriation of the capitalist bourgeoisie.

Can they pretend to be unaware that what they unjustly call thievery really should be called savings, and that savings is the basis of any society?

One must acknowledge that some of these utopians, those who do not try to focus their ambitions on the political field, might have been or are of good faith. These people have spread their ideas by the pen or spoken word. They have not substituted a bomb for a book, nor have they preached propaganda through deeds; they were only anarchists in theory, never in practice.

Kaw-djer must be classed among the latter people. He was never implicated in the anarchist violence that marked the end of the nineteenth century.

An untamed, indomitable, stubborn spirit, who tolerated no authority, incapable of obedience, rebelling against all the laws, which despite their doubtless imperfections, are necessary for people to live among one another.

The anarchists have never wished to recognize this necessity, because they campaign for the destruction of all laws, while advocating theories of absolute individuality, and struggle to abolish social relationships.

Such were the doctrines of this foreigner, who came from a place unknown, as a voluntary exile in these distant regions, who from an immense need to be charitable had consecrated his life to the Indians, who greeted him with the name of "benefactor"! He was like a Saint Vincent de Paul combined with a Lassalle, for Kaw-djer was a good soul, lost in the most forward-moving systems of collectivity, being one of those who feels that any means are justifiable in perfecting social government.

And just as he rejected any human authority, he also rejected all divine authority, as he was an anarchist atheist, which makes perfect sense. As we have seen, he brandished the motto, which he had spoken on top of the Fuegian cliff, where he seemed to embrace heaven and earth:

"Neither God nor master!"

Faced by such beliefs, which never wavered, was there reason to hope that one day this man's spirit would change and he would recognize the falsehood and danger of doctrines that are in total contradiction with the needs of social order; and that society must always be based on social inequality, a basic law of nature, which must apply to humanity as well; and that finally, if justice and absolute equality are not to be found in this world, that at least they exist in the next world?

Perhaps, at the time when he sought to leave his country—and maybe this was one of the motivating factors—he witnessed the socialist party slide toward disorganization, and hostilities break out among warring brethren. Perhaps he saw that it was impossible for the ideas he had devoted his life to, to ever succeed. Perhaps he despaired of ever attaining the goal he had always advanced toward, unflinchingly.

Disgusted by contact with his fellow man and becoming horrified by them—not driven from France, Germany, Britain, or the United States—but disgusted by their so-called civilization, impatient to shake off the burden of any authority whatsoever, he sought a corner of the earth where man could still live in total independence. He believed he had found it in the middle of this archipelago at the limits of the inhabited world, which belonged to no power. With its sparse and disconnected tribes, Magellania offered him something at the ends of southern America that he could not have found in Europe, Asia, or Africa, and not even in the Oceanian islands.

So he sold all of his belongings, for a modest fortune, secretly left Ireland, his latest residence, and traveled anonymously on a ship headed for the Falklands, waiting for an occasion to reach one of the Magellanian Islands; debarking on the southern coast of Tierra del Fuego, he led the life we have seen amid the Yacana Indians, a wandering life which led him from campground to campground, as hunter and fisherman, and above all, doing good deeds to help the poor natives, with his tireless sense of charity.

We also know the situation that led Kaw-djer to move to New Island, where he lived for the past six years with the pilot Karroly and his son, Halg. His only hope and desire was that nothing would happen to disturb his solitary and calm refuge, at the threshold of which he might have inscribed: *Sollicitae jucunda oblivia vitae* ["Fortunate forgettings of a tormented life," a tag from the Latin poet Horace].

Then came the treaty of 1881 signed by Chile and Argentina. The division of Patagonia and Magellania made them lose the independence they had enjoyed until then. After this treaty, Chile owned the entire portion of Magellanian territories located to the south of Beagle Canal. No part of the archipelago escaped the rule of the governor of Punta Arenas, not even New Island upon which Kaw-djer had found asylum.

Kaw-djer, who had retreated to his room, was seated with his head in his hands in front of a small table, still not recovered from the shock he had just received, in the way lightning strikes a mighty tree and shakes it to the roots.

Finally, he rose and took a few steps toward the window and opened it, noticing that Karroly and his son stood motionless at the foot of the hillock. They turned to him, but he didn't call them . . .

His thoughts were on the future—a future that no longer offered any security. Representatives would be sent to the island.

They would know that he lived there. He was aware that several times officialdom had been concerned about the presence of the foreigner in Magellania, where he was located in the archipelago, his contacts with the natives, and the influence he might use... The Chilean governor wanted to question him, to learn his identity, and dig into his past life, forcing him to abandon the incognito that he prized above everything else . . .

Some days passed. Kaw-djer said nothing more about the changes made by the treaty of division. But he was more somber than ever. What was he thinking about? Was he considering leaving New Island, separating from his faithful Indian and the boy for whom he felt such deep affection? But where would he go? In what other corner of the earth would he find independence, without which he seemed unable to exist? Even if he took refuge on the remotest Magellanian rocks, on the Cape Horn islet, could he escape the Chilean authorities? Or would he need to go farther, still farther, always farther, until he reached the uninhabited territories of Antarctica?

It was the beginning of February. Good weather would last for another two months, the season in which Kaw-djer would visit the Fuegian campgrounds, before winter made the Beagle Canal and the archipelago's sounds unnavigable.

However, he did not prepare to embark on the longboat. The unrigged *Wel-kiej* stayed at the back of the cove. There did not even seem to be any vessel in sight of the island, and Karroly had no piloting to do. The Indian was somewhat afraid of going away. He sensed what was going on in Kaw-djer's mind, the struggle occurring inside him. Karroly could not leave him alone, facing such frightful discouragement. He feared not finding him there when he got back.

Finally, on the afternoon of February seventh, Kaw-djer climbed to the top of the bluff, and looked to the west. He was motionless, perhaps looking to see if some Chilean vessel, such as the sloop anchored at Punta Arenas, was coming along the canal in the direction of New Island. He saw nothing to confirm his fears, and yet, when he returned to the seashore, he told Karroly:

"Clear the longboat for tomorrow as early as possible."

"A trip of several days?" asked the Indian.

"Yes!" Kaw-djer replied.

Karroly called his son and set to work immediately. He only had until the end of the day to equip the *Wel-kiej*, bringing sails and tackle, with equipment and provisions needed for a trip that doubtless would last for a week. Had Kaw-djer decided to return to the midst of the Fuegian tribes before the inclement season? Would he revisit Tierra del Fuego, which had become an Argentinean possession? Did he wish to see the Pecherais one last time before abandoning them forever? Karroly did not inquire about these matters.

"Will Halg be accompanying us?" was all that he asked.

"Yes."

"And the dog?"

"Zol, too."

That was Kaw-djer's entire response.

Toward the evening, the preparations were completed. As usual, provisions had been loaded aboard the longboat along with fishing and hunting equipment.

The next day at dawn, the *Wel-kiej* set out. The wind blew from the east in a stormy gale. Fairly strong undertow beat upon the rocks at the foot of the bluff. To the north, the open sea rose up in wide surges.

If Kaw-djer intended to reach Tierra del Fuego from the side of Le Maire Straits, the longboat would have to struggle, for the wind increased as the sun rose on the horizon. This was not the case, for on his orders, after having turned around the farthest point of New Island, the longboat headed toward Navarin Island, whose double peaks blurred indistinctly in the morning fog from the west.

Before sunset that day, the *Wel-kiej* put in at the southern point of the island, one of the middle points of the Magellanic Archipelago, in the back of a little cove with a sheer bank, where it would be guaranteed a night's calm.

For an hour, Karroly and his son caught some fine fish with their lines and collected a number of mollusks on the rocks. They might have hunted sea lions and other amphibians that sported on the shore. But what would they have done with the carcasses, if the longboat delayed returning to New Island? And they did not know what Kaw-djer's plans were. The latter, still deep in thought, kept absolutely quiet, as if he were transfixed by an obsession. Motionless, at the base of the forward mast, he made no move to debark. He did not even stretch out on the upper deck, but remained in this position until morning.

All of the next day was spent on this part of the island.

While Karroly and Halg were busy with different tasks, such as cleaning the longboat and stocking up on fish and mollusks, Kaw-djer descended to the shore. But he had no intention of hunting, for he did not bring Zol, and left his gun aboard, even though marine prey pullulated on the shore. No doubt he wanted to see, perhaps for the last time, some places on Navarin Island that he had already visited several times, like its neighbor, Hoste Island. It was deserted at this time, or more accurately—since no Indians made their home there—no campgrounds were visible, and it seemed as if the sea lion hunters had not been there for some time.

For a good part of the day, Kaw-djer wandered through solitary prairies and silent forest depths. When he climbed a hill whose summit emerged from the greenery, he paused and looked out to the entire visible portion of the sea. From there, to the south, he glimpsed a confusion of other islands, to the southeast Lennox and the islets surrounding it, and vast Nassau Bay, which indented Hoste Island so deeply. Perhaps, he told himself, that beyond here the channels grew wider, the archipelago was divided more and more, the sea beat upon nothing but reefs, and that for himself, a wandering fugitive, there would be no more land beyond Cape Horn.

When evening fell, Kaw-djer, back aboard, ate dinner with the others. Still withdrawn, he barely answered the infrequent questions from the Indian and his son, those two beings who were so attached to him, and for whom he felt deep affection. For a moment, he looked at them, and it seemed as if he might tell them why he had left New Island, and why he was headed toward the waters where the Atlantic Ocean meets the Pacific.

The next day, after a calm night, the longboat weighed anchor, cut across Nassau Bay obliquely, and steered for Wollaston Island at its southern end. The sea there was fairly rough. The bay was covered to the west by the high cliffs of Hoste Island and the Evout Islets that emerge from the southeast; the longboard was frightfully battered by the open sea's swells in the section between these islets and the Lennox Islets. Kaw-djer had to take the helm while Karroly and Halg kept alert with the foresail and the mainsail, for they had to maneuver against a fairly strong breeze that required taking in a reef.

In the evening, the *Wel-kiej* found its berth on the northern tip of Wollaston Island, which was projected into Nassau Bay.

This island, indented on its coastline and with wide plains in its interior, did not offer the strong contrasts of Hoste and Navarin. It was two to three times smaller, and its rivers flowed calmly on the surface. But its prairies, surrounded by antarctic trees and abundant grasses, made it apt for raising livestock, and surely the Chilean government would exploit it, as Great Britain did with the Falklands, by founding agricultural establishments there.

The longboat had not been jolted too much, sheltered as it was on the other side of the promontory against the violent undertow that struck from the east. Kaw-djer wanted to spend the night at the back of an anfractuosity where a litter of dried kelp was piled up. He could fall asleep there better than he could on the top deck of the *Wel-kiej.* Karroly felt tragic forebodings and did not think of sleeping for a moment. On several occasions, when the sea's lapping drowned out his footsteps, he debarked to the shore to assure himself that Kaw-djer was still stretched out in the cave.

Around three A.M., the Indian saw him on the shore and went to him.

"Leave me alone, my friend," Kaw-djer said in a gentle, sad voice. "Leave me alone and go rest until daybreak."

Karroly went back aboard, while Kaw-djer, climbing back up the foreland, went toward the island's interior. He reappeared around eleven o'clock for the morning meal, and around five o'clock for the evening meal.

But the weather was growing stormy. The breeze picked up from the northeast. Thick clouds accumulated on the horizon. A storm threatened. As the longboat continued in a southerly direction, it was important to choose channels where the sea would be less violent. That's what was done upon leaving Wollaston Island. Karroly went to the west, between it and Baily Island, and skirted the western portion so as to wind up in the straits that separate Hermitte Island from Herschell Island.

This whole group makes up what is called the Cape Horn Archipelago, of which Wollaston Island is the main one, amid Grevy, Baily, Freycinet, Hermitte, Herschell, and Deceit Islands, as well as Wood, Waterman, Hope, Henderson, Ildefonso, and Barnevelt Islets, of which the farthest granite one marked the fearsome Cape Horn.

When we examine the map of this wracked area, broken as if a fall had smashed it into a thousand pieces, we must feel as Dumont d'Urville did when he said: "When one contemplates these marvelous accidents of earth, the imagination involuntarily goes to the globe's turning, whose powerful force broke the southern part of America into pieces and gave it the form of that archipelago named Tierra del Fuego, but what did nature use to get these results—fire, water, or just polar movement?"

The question is still where the illustrious French seaman left it, and no geographers or geologists can give any answer yet.

It wasn't to solve this problem that Kaw-djer went down to the archipelago's farthest islets, which had now become property of the Chilean republic. No, it was only too clear that he sought to flee these subjugated waters, refusing to tread on ground that was no longer free. But what would he do when he reached the extreme limits of the earth, arrived at Cape Horn, and saw only the immense ocean before him?

On the afternoon of February fifteenth, the longboat put into port at the end of the archipelago, braving extreme danger, amid a sea tossed with hurricane-like violence. All of Karroly's skill and intelligence were required to choose the most sheltered channels to avoid sinking or smashing against the reefs. Kaw-djer barely noticed the dangers run by the *Wel-kiej*, and had he been alone amid the shocks of the gale, he might have wanted to sink in the swirling of the two oceans at the base of Cape Horn . . .

The longboat found shelter at the back of a narrow cove, at the island's southern edge. Karroly and his son took care to berth it firmly, after putting the grappling iron ashore. Then the sails were left on their brails, as the port call would doubtless be brief.

When Kaw-djer debarked, he said nothing about his plans, sent back the dog that tried to follow him, and headed for the foreland, leaving Karroly and Halg on the shore.

Horn Island is made up almost completely of a chaotic agglomeration of enormous rocks strewn at the base with floating wood, and gigantic sea-tangle brought by the waves. Above, hundreds of tips of the reef emerged from the sparkling undertow.

The foreland was only around six hundred meters above sea level. It was an enormous rock, rounded at the top, which was easily climbed on its rear side to the north, with very gradual slopes like those that climb in long curves around the Rock of Gibraltar. But this was a reversed Gibraltar, with its vertical side facing the sea.

After following the shore for seven or eight hundred steps, Kaw-djer climbed one of the footpaths in order to reach the foreland's highest point. Sometimes the climb was difficult, with a very steep incline, and he had to cling to lapidary clumps set into the chinks of humus. Small landslides caused stones to bounce down the foreland's slope.

What would Kaw-djer do up there? Did he want to see to the farthest limits of the southern horizon? But there was nothing to see but the immense sheet of ocean that extended, for more than eleven degrees, up to the Antarctic Circle.

As he climbed higher, Kaw-djer was more violently assaulted by the squall. The air, full of water molecules, enveloped and went through him as if it were blowing out of a powerful ventilator. If his garment were not tied to his waist, it would have been reduced to shreds. But nothing stopped his steady climb.

Below, the Indian and Halg noticed his silhouette gradually growing smaller. They saw him struggle against the gusty winds. They wondered if they should join him, to help and accompany him to the peak where perhaps no human foot had ever stood before. But Kaw-djer had not told them to follow him, so they stayed on the shore.

The difficult climb took fully two and a half hours, and it was nearly seven o'clock when Kaw-djer reached the foreland's summit.

He went up to the highest ridge, and there in the midst of the gale, he stood motionless, looking toward the south.

Night was starting to fall in the east, but the opposite horizon was still lit by the last rays from the sun, which flushed the sky and water. Heavy clouds, sent awry by the winds into tatters of vapor that spun out in the gale, went by with a hurricane's speed.

Before his eyes was nothing but the immense spread of sea upon which no reef appeared, and from atop the foreland [. . .] leagues away, the Diego Ramirez Islets were invisible.

Finally, what had this man whose soul was so deeply troubled come here to do? Had he already decided to do away with himself? Did he tell himself that he would carry on ahead so long as the earth, which he no longer wanted anything to do with, was under his feet—yet still feel the desire to seek death in the waves that broke over its farthest reaches? All he had to do was throw himself from atop the foreland; in these deep waters, he would not even strike any underwater rocks, and his body would be a victim of two oceans.

Yes! That's what he had resolved, now that he was dispossessed of his last refuge on Magellanic territory.

"Neither God nor master!" he shouted at this supreme moment.

And he started to throw himself into the void, when a distant lightning bolt crossed the sky, followed by an explosion.

It was a cannon shot from a ship in distress on the open sea at Cape Horn.

VIII

THE SHIPWRECK

It was 7:30 P.M. On the sea's surface, weighed down by heavy clouds, night fell heavily, almost without dusk, as if the sun suddenly went out. It could no longer be felt on the side where it was presently going down, and it was doubtful if the breaking waves were still topped by a radiant crest.

The wind blew from the southeast, meeting no obstacle on this open immensity, and beat to one side with remarkable violence. That night, any vessel that tried to go around the farthest point of America would surely have risked being lost.

The ship in distress was threatened with just this danger, which the warning shot signified. Certainly, it was possible for it to pass between Cape Horn and the Diego Ramirez Islets, which were separated by an arm of sea, but only if it had sufficient sails to raise against the wind. Amid the increasing squalls and blinding gusts, with clouds seeming to rush down in an avalanche, could the vessel maintain enough sail to keep running and heaving to?

How could it withstand such atmospheric outbursts, and if it was a sailboat, might its masts and spars not be disabled?

A second cannon shot resounded. The violent artillery explosion looked like a missile.

Kaw-djer was no longer alone at the top of the islet. At the sound of the explosions, the Indian and his son, after leaving the longboat well berthed, quickly arrived at the plateau by hanging on agilely to the foreland's rocks by the clumps that grew in the fissures.

The rain fell no longer, although a liquid mist impregnated the air, with spray from the undertow flying up to that height.

Intermittently, the vessel could be seen across the floating haze, as the squall drove it to the coastline. It was a large four-master, whose black hull, rolling from side to side, stood out against the white sea swells. The vessel came from the west, fighting contrary winds.

"They will not get around," said Karroly.

"No," replied Kaw-djer, "the sea is too difficult and the current is dragging them under . . ."

"Do they know they are close to land, and do they see the coastline from this distance?" continued the Indian.

"He can't have seen it amid this darkness," stated Kaw-djer, "for if he had seen it, and knowing that the wind is pushing him there, he would head for the open sea . . ."

"Can he do that," asked Karroly, "if he hasn't maintained his sails? It looks like he only has his topsails in the low reefs! If he doesn't take advantage of a change of wind, he will be thrown against the foreland's rocks!"

How could this vessel benefit from changes of wind? It only varied by a few rhumbs and always heaved to the south. Surely, no one aboard, whether officer or crewman, knew that land was so close, or that the storm was carrying them there abruptly. If so, they would have fled to the southwest.

At this moment, in the middle of one of those silent interruptions that punctuate squalls, a number of crackings were heard, and had the vessel been closer, one would have thought it was breaking up against the reefs.

"They are lost," shouted Karroly.

Indeed, the two mizzenmasts broke off at the step, dragging the tackle down with their fall. As the crew was unable to set up storm jibs, the vessel no longer had any sails at the stern. It could no longer face the wind while heaving to go up the coastline. As the wind blew full southerly, it had to sink, unless it could run onto one of the channels to the left or right of the foreland.

Two more cannon shots were heard over the gale, and this time, the vessel was more than a mile and a half from shore. What help could they expect in the middle of these waters? Doubtless, they were aware that they were in the waters of Cape Horn, which was recognizable even amid the night's gloom.

It was necessary to show them the foreland, which they hadn't seen, and indicate their definite position so that they could fend off the reefs, and perhaps find shelter in the Magellanian canals, either on the side of Herschell Island, or Hermitte Island where the sea would be more tractable.

"A fire! . . . A fire!" shouted Kaw-djer.

"Come," said the Indian to his son.

Both of them went to collect armfuls of dried branches on the slopes of the foreland, torn from the shrubbery with which it bristled, long grass that the winds had piled up in the anfractuosities, and kelp that was hanging between the rocks. In all haste, they collected this combustible material at the top of the enormous crest and made a hearth of it.

However, new explosions echoed two or three times within the island. Kaw-djer gauged from their sharper sound that the ship was already within a mile of shore.

It was eight o'clock. The sea disappeared beneath a deep gloom, swept by the gusts from the squall.

Kaw-djer struck the flint. The tinder caught fire, the brushwood lit up, and the flame, animated by the atmospheric flow, quickly engulfed the whole hearth, which went up as if fed by the bellows of a mighty ventilator.

In less than a minute, a column of flame stood on the top of the foreland, twisting as it projected an intense light, while the smoke curled to the north in thick whirls. The storm's roaring was accompanied by the crackling of wood as timber hitches burst like cartridges exposed to a spark. Once more, amid the darkness split by explosions, the Magellanic waters deserved the name of Tierra del Fuego.

Cape Horn would be an ideal place for a lighthouse to brighten the dangerous approaches on the border between two oceans. This lighthouse will necessarily be built one day. The security of navigation demands it. Already, Ile des Etats sends off night flares at Vancouver Point; but these are remote and are only of use to ships coming from the east across the Atlantic.

There is no doubt that the hearth lit by Kaw-djer was seen. Aboard the ship in distress, they must have been aware that the shore was only a mile away under the lee, and the storm was pushing them in that direction. The captain had to know that he was abeam of Cape Horn, if he had measured his position during the day. No doubt he had tried to get around it; but pushed back by the wind and driven by the currents, the ship was unable to haul itself out to the open sea. Now, half disabled, the only salvation was to throw itself across the channels on both sides of Cape Horn.

This maneuver was highly dangerous in such deep darkness. Kaw-djer and Karroly only glimpsed the ship through the light of cannon firings. Although the foreland's bluffs were free, reefs were abundant once past the headland. Who but someone accustomed to these waters could manage to steer and shelter behind the island? And even then, could he do so during the dark hours that would go by before daybreak? . . .

However, the hearth continued to throw out sparks through the night. Karroly and Halg continually fed it. There was enough combustible material to last until morning if need be.

Kaw-djer, standing in front of the hearth while the flames curved behind it, tried to gauge the ship's position. He pondered what it would take to help it, prevent its collision against the reefs, and guide it through the channels. Now he no longer thought of ending his own life, but saving the unfortunate people threatened with death. By the firelight, when he turned to the Indian and his son, he saw they were ready to obey him.

"On board!" he finally shouted.

All three rushed daringly down the foreland's slope, reaching the shore in a few minutes, and with the dog following, they embarked in the longboat. With the grappling hook aboard, they emerged from the cove, with Halg at the rudder, and Kaw-djer and Karroly manning the oars; it was impossible to put the smallest bit of sail out, or the wind would have thrown the *Wel-kiej* off to the north.

They needed to get past the reefs that laterally covered the base of the foreland, against which the squall broke with indescribable fury. Piercing shrieks of birds went over amid the spindrifts.

It was with great difficulty that the longboat freed itself from the reefs' whirlpools, even though the oars were handled by powerful rowers. Outside, the sea was raging. The waves broke with a furious din, as if they were hitting bottom, although the sounding line measured several hundred feet deep. The *Wel-kiej*, shaken almost to pieces, leapt up, twisting around from side to side, upended itself sometimes, as seamen say, with its entire stem out of the water, then fell back again weightily. Heavy parcels of sea embarked, crashed with a shower on the upper deck, and rolled to the back of the boat. Weighed down by this burden of water, the longboat ran the risk of sinking. Halg had to leave the rudder and, bailer in hand, scooped out the water that otherwise would have filled the well deck. The brave boy did the task deftly, while adjusting the tiller from time to time. He had learned the difficult pilot's trade in the channels of the Magellanic Archipelago.

The longboat went as straight as possible toward the ship, whose riding lights could finally be seen. Indeed, driven by the gale, it approached all the more rapidly. In a few minutes, Kaw-djer and his companions would be alongside it.

The great shape could be seen, which pitched like a giant buoy, blacker than the sea and the sky. Its two back masts, held in place by their backstays, followed in tow, while the foremast and mainmast moved in forty-five-degree arcs, ripping through the fog.

The danger was that the masts, raised up by the sea swell, might plunge into the ship's hull, smashing it.

"What is the captain doing?" shouted Karroly, "and why hasn't he got rid of them yet? He can't drag that tail through the channels!"

Kaw-djer did not reply. He thought that perhaps the ship's officers and crew were panicked, or perhaps the captain was no longer aboard.

Indeed, it was most urgent to cut the tackle that held on to the masts, which had fallen into the sea. But doubtless chaos reigned aboard and no one had thought of this. No orders or maneuvering seemed to be occurring. Not a single man was seen running along the rails, or hoisting himself up on the ratlines of the two masts that were still standing.

However, the crew had to be aware that the vessel was being hauled down below sea level, that only ten or so cables held it together, and it would soon sink. The fiery hearth on the crest of Cape Horn still threw off some tongues of flame, which wavered disproportionately as the blaze was moved by the gale force.

"Is there no one left on board?" asked the Indian, as if seconding Kaw-djer's thought.

Yes, the ship might have been abandoned by its passengers, officers and crew, and these unfortunate people, before they could jump into small boats, might have been taken up in the wash of two oceans, whose flux and reflux made the Cape Horn waters so dangerous and sometimes unnavigable. During brief lulls, no shouts were heard, no desperate calls for help. The vessel might be transformed into a giant coffin, containing the dead and dying, whose bodies would soon be torn against the reefs.

Finally, the *Wel-kiej* arrived alongside the ship just when it yawed to starboard and almost went under. Karroly hit the tiller, which allowed them to glide beside the hull, which had pieces of hawser and rope hanging from it. The Indian skillfully grabbed one of them and, with a single motion, made it fast to the longboat's portside.

Then his son and himself, with Kaw-djer following, climbed up this hawser, went over the handrails, and landed on the deck.

No! The ship had not been abandoned. A frantic crowd of passengers—men and women and children—cluttered it. There were several hundred unfortunate and terrified people, mostly stretched out against the deckhouses along the gangways, who were unable to stand upright due to the unbearable rollings.

In the darkness, no one noticed the two men and a boy who had just pulled up along the hull and jumped over the bulwark on the other side of the foremast.

Karroly hurried to the stern, hoping to find the helmsman at his post.

The helm had been abandoned. The ship, out of sail, ran where the wind and swells took it.

But where were the captain and other officers? Had they abjectly abandoned ship, disregarding their duty?

Kaw-djer grabbed a sailor by the arm and asked him in English, "Your commander?"

The man didn't even seem to realize that a stranger was speaking to him, although Kaw-djer's face was lit up by the Cape Horn fire, and all he did was shrug his shoulders.

"Your commander?" Kaw-djer repeated.

"Slung overboard with a dozen others, along with the masts."

So the ship no longer had a captain and was also lacking part of its crew.

"Second in command?" asked Kaw-djer.

Again the sailor shrugged, indifferent or rather resigned to whatever might happen.

He replied, "The second? Hauled down to steerage with both legs broken."

"But the lieutenant? Petty officers? Where are they?"

The sailor made a gesture to show that he didn't know.

"Well, who is in command aboard ship?" shouted Kaw-djer.

"You are!" answered Karroly, who had just joined him.

"To the helm, then," ordered Kaw-djer, "and let's head for the channel!"

He and Karroly ran as fast as they could to the stern, and with hands on the wheel, tried to steer the boat to the west of Cape Horn.

What was this boat? Where was it headed? We will learn that later. As for its name and home port, these could be read on the wheel, by the light of a lantern brought by Halg:

JONATHAN—SAN FRANCISCO.

The violent yaws made the rudder very hard to maneuver. Unfortunately, it had little effect, as the ship was not moving at the right speed and drifted with the swell.

However, Kaw-djer and Karroly tried to keep it in the direction of the channel. The Cape Horn fire still let out a few flames, but it would soon be extinguished.

But it would take more than a few minutes to reach the entry of the canal that divided Hermitte and Horn Islands on the portside. If the ship managed to clear some reefs that emerged midway there, perhaps it would arrive at a moorage sheltered from wind and sea. They could wait there in security until daybreak.

First, an indispensable precaution was taken. Karroly, helped by some sailors, went to the stern. They barely noticed that an Indian was commanding them. They rushed to cut the starboard shrouds and backstays that held on to the two trailing masts. It was vital to avoid violent shocks. Although the hull was made of iron, it might have been smashed in.

The tackle was hacked free and Karroly saw that the masts and spars were left to drift away, causing no more problems. As for the longboat, the *Wel-kiej*, its stopper brought it to portside in a way that prevented any collision. Next, Karroly returned to the helm.

The waves' fury grew near the reefs, and enormous waves came over the handrails. The passengers had a new reason for panic and fright. They would have been better off sheltered under the deckhouses or 'tween decks. But how to communicate with these unfortunate folk! There was no chance, with some knocked over by swells and rolled from one side of the ship to the other.

Finally, the ship got around the cape, after some terrifying yaws exposing one and then another of its sides to the sea's attack, skirted the reefs that bristled on the west, and went along Horn Island, whose heights, overlooking anfractuous coves, protected it partly from the squall's violence. It was almost smashed. A bit of sail was hoisted from the bow instead of a jib. Karroly tried to hold a course at the helm, with some other men beside him, including the ship's mate.

To the latter, he had simply declared: "Pilot!" and the other man did not ask any further questions.

All danger was not past, and when the vessel would arrive at the northern part of the island and be hit by contrary winds, it would again be exposed to the entire violence of the waves and wind that strung along the arm of sea between Horn Island and Herschell Island. But it was impossible to avoid this channel, since the cape's coastline offered no shelter, not a single bight where *The Jonathan* could put in its anchors. Moreover, the wind, heading farther and farther south, would soon make that part of the archipelago unnavigable.

However, Kaw-djer hoped that Karroly might be able, thanks to his pilot's skill and instincts, to head west to the southern coastline of Hermitte Island, finding shelter in the Hall Islets, which was possible if the rudder held steady. The open coastline was around a dozen miles long, offering points of shelter. On the other side of one of its extremities, inside a cove removed from swells, *The Jonathan* would be safe until the storm's end, whether it came in twenty-four or forty-eight hours. When the sea was calm again and the winds favorable, Karroly would try to go up to Beagle Canal, between Hoste and Navarin Islands, and even though the vessel was nearly disabled, to take it to Punta Arenas through the Magellan Straits.

But what dangers faced the navigation up to Hermitte Island! How to avoid the numerous reefs scattered throughout the channels? With the sails reduced to a bit of jib that might be blown away at any moment, how to assure the vessel's advance amid the deep gloom?

Finally, after a frightful hour, the last rocks of Horn Island were bypassed, and the vessel was washed powerfully by the sea. It came with such force on to one deck and then the other that the jib no longer functioned. The first mate, aided by a dozen sailors, tried to set a trysail on the foremast.

It was a storm jib of thick canvas with solid bolt-ropes at its edges, which strained against the powerful tempest. It would be difficult to hoist it right up to the foremast rigging, where neither shrouds nor stays had given way, board the tack of the sail and haul it tight downwind.

It took a full half hour to manage it. After a thousand difficulties, with the canvas cracking like the sound of gunfire, the sail was put into place and held there by pulley blocks, which took all of the men's strength. Certainly for a vessel of its weight, this bit of canvas action would usually be barely perceptible. However it was felt, considering the wind's power, and the seven or eight miles that separated Horn Island and Hermitte Island were covered in less than an hour.

Kaw-djer and Karroly hoped that *The Jonathan* could reach the other side of the headland that projected to the south, and find shelter there, when a little before ten o'clock, a frightful cracking could be heard amid the squall's roar.

The foremast had just broken off at about ten feet above the bridge. It fell, dragging with it part of the mainmast, whose tackle gave way, and topmasts, topgallants, and yards disappeared, crushing the portside handrails.

This disaster killed several of the passengers and crew, who let out heartrending screams. At the same moment, *The Jonathan* listed so far that it almost capsized, after taking on an enormous amount of water.

The ship righted itself, as a torrent flooded from stem to stern, between the gangways, falling down the scupperholes, and across the broken handrails. Fortunately, the tackle was broken, and the debris carried by the swell no longer endangered the hull.

Soon *The Jonathan* no longer responded to its rudder and began to go adrift.

"We're lost!" shouted one of the sailors.

"And no small craft!" shouted another.

Indeed, they had been carried off by the sea.

"There's the pilot's longboat!" shouted a third man.

All of them rushed aft, where the *Wel-kiej* followed in its wake.

"Stop!" ordered Kaw-djer, and this command was given in such an imperious voice that the first mate and his men had to obey.

They just waited for the final outcome, which is to say, the final catastrophe. If *The Jonathan* missed Hermitte Island, maybe the rising tide's currents would carry them westward, and they would break up against the Santo Ildefonso Islets. Deprived of its mast, what would become of the ship in the fearsome Pacific Ocean?

An hour later, Karroly glimpsed an enormous body. It was Wollaston Island whose peaks were dimly outlined to the north. But the current made itself felt in the channels where the eastern swells whirled round, and Wollaston Island was almost immediately passed on the starboard side.

A little before midnight, *The Jonathan* was about to pass between Hermitte Island and the foreground of Hoste Island, when a powerful shock rocked it to its very framework. It stopped abruptly, listing to portside.

The American ship had just put in on the coastline at the tip of Hoste Island, known as False Cape Horn.

IX

THE JONATHAN

Two weeks before the night of February fifteenth to sixteenth, the American clipper *The Jonathan* left San Francisco, California, heading for southern Africa. It was a crossing of [. . .] miles, that a fast ship might make in five weeks, given favorable winds and seas.

This sailboat, with a burden of 2,500 tons, was equipped with four masts, the foremast and mainmast with square sails, and the two others with lateen sails, spankers and topsails. It was built in the Sherry and Foster shipyards. Rated as a first-class vessel, with a finely elongated iron hull, its draft, perfect sails and masts, and machinery for various onboard functions, offered every assurance of a quick crossing.

She was commanded by Captain Leccar, an excellent seaman in his prime, and under his orders were the first mate Musgrave, lieutenants Furner and Maddison, boatswain Tom Sand, and a crew of twenty-seven men, all Americans.

The Jonathan had already crossed the Pacific Ocean twice, headed for Australia and British East India. Its returns from Calcutta and Sydney were made under favorable conditions, even though the southern seas were violent as usual. From both a maritime and business point of view, its owners, Blount and Frary, were pleased with the results of these two trips.

For this latest trip, which had just finished in catastrophe, *The*

Jonathan was not chartered to transport merchandise. Nine hundred emigrants had boarded it, headed for a southern African colony. This colony would be established on a land grant accorded by the Portuguese government at Lagoa Bay, part of South Africa's Portuguese possessions.

Most of these emigrants were from the northern states. However, they also included some German and Irish families, the sort of Americanized Europeans who are plentiful in Illinois and California. The colonization company, which opened in these states, invited emigrants of every origin to populate the vast land grants obtained on Lagoa Bay, in a fertile land, in the hopes of offsetting British influence on the Cape.

To amalgamate this hybrid population made up of diverse elements would be difficult if the severe discipline that they experienced aboard *The Jonathan* were not repeated on land. The four-master had been outfitted for transporting the colonists. Men, women, and children were able to settle down fairly comfortably inside the deckhouse and steerage. The crossing was not meant to take a long time. In February and March, after going down the American coastline, *The Jonathan* faced the warm season, and in neither the Pacific nor the Atlantic would she encounter the extreme bad weather of wintertime.

Apart from provisions needed for the trip, the clipper's cargo included everything the colony would need at its beginnings. Several months' worth of flour, canned food, and alcoholic drinks ensured that the nine hundred emigrants would be fed. *The Jonathan* also carried equipment for a first settlement, like tents, collapsible dwellings, scant furniture, and necessary household utensils. The company took care to provide colonists agricultural equipment that would allow them to immediately exploit the land grants: different varieties of plants, seeds for sowing, grains and vegetables, a certain number of livestock of the bovine, porcine, and ovine species, all the usual farmyard breeds. Guns and ammunition were also included, in case it was necessary to fight off attacks from the Namaquas and Boshimans, who were still warring with the other Hottentot tribes. Therefore, the new colony's fate was assured for a sufficient time. In any case, it would not be abandoned to its own devices. After returning to San Francisco, *The Jonathan* would bring a second cargo that would complete the first one, and if the project seemed to be a success, would transport a second group of colonists to Lagoa Bay. There is no shortage of poor souls whose lives are too difficult, or even impossible in their motherland, so that they devote all their energies to creating a new one in a foreign land.

The trip's start was not auspicious. No sooner had they cast off, after being laid up in San Francisco and before reaching the latitude of San Digeo (lower California), *The Jonathan* had to struggle against contrary winds from the southwest. Captain Leccar decided to head for the open sea, rather than risk sinking. A few days later, they had to face extremely violent winds and got to the cape by way of Cape Corrientes, at the latitude of Mexico.

The emigrants on the clipper, settled into cramped conditions, suffered considerably during bad weather when they could not stay up on deck. But finally *The Jonathan* was not seriously damaged, and after having scudded to the west for a few days, regained her course toward the Galapagos cluster of islands, which is across from Ecuador.

The sailing continued, interrupted both by calms and storms. The passengers' moods reflected the weather. There were threats and complaints. Captain Leccar, well seconded by his first mate Musgrave, had to take strong measures to check mutinous attempts. Among the emigrants were disorderly men, adventurers ready to go too far, which was hardly assuring for the new colony's future.

Unsurprisingly, amid this varied population were some professional revolutionaries, always battling with the law, enemies of any social order, agents of chaos, who were tolerated by no country's police. Among the most fearsome were the Irish-born brothers John and Jack Merritt, who belonged to the Fenyans sect, against which England had to take draconian measures. Expelled from the United Kingdom, which usually shows an imprudent tolerance for any other country's agitators, these two brothers, aged forty and forty-five, signed up among the emigrants whom the clipper was transporting to southern Africa. What was their plan, and what would they do at Lagoa Bay? Perhaps start trouble for their own profit, or perhaps impose their own ideas there. Although propagandists in point of fact, they were quite different from Kaw-djer, whose doctrine rejected violence.

These anarchists didn't even wait for *The Jonathan* to reach its destination. Amid the few hundred passengers, they found a certain number who were willing to be influenced by them, unfortunate people whose poverty exposed them to all sorts of evil incitement. Certainly, the large majority of emigrants resisted their attempt to contravene shipboard discipline. On several occasions Captain Leccar was obliged to intervene energetically, to thwart the agitators.

The Jonathan continued to travel down the Pacific waters, much tested by the frequent squalls on the open sea. Fortunately, they met trade winds in these waters, located on both sides of the equator between the thirtieth parallel north and south. No doubt due to the diurnal movement of the sun, they blew from east to west, but spread steadily and regularly, never developing into a mighty wind or powerful breeze, and the clipper progressed southward by hugging the coastline. There was no need to make a tack on the open sea. They followed the American coastline, sometimes ten miles away and sometimes thirty, from the latitude of Lima, Peru to Valparaiso, Chile, at medium speed, even though they nearly always had to fight violent seas. By February eleventh, they were only ten degrees or six hundred nautical miles away from Cape Pilares, at the western entrance to the Magellan Straits.

Captain Leccar intended to cross the straits to get from the Pacific Ocean to the Atlantic. As is well known, the straits are a better route for steam vessels than sailboats. The latter may hesitate to enter, as many changes of direction are required, following the movement of channels, which are easy maneuvers for steamers.

When a sailboat appears from the west, it has an easier time. It has already left the region of trade winds that blow from the east, and as mentioned, the main winds in the Magellan Straits are from west to east, or from Cape Pilares to Cape des Vierges. A clipper like *The Jonathan* had every incentive to take this path, where she would encounter steady breezes, allowing her to avoid the turbulent waters of Cape Horn.

After arriving at the fifty-second degree of latitude, the captain went along the west coast of Adelaide Island, from Cape Isabel to Cape Parker, in order to arrive at the straits after avoiding the dangers of the Sir John Narborough Archipelago. Cape Pilares remained directly to the east, at the edge of Tierra del Desolation.

As we know, between these two land masses, or rather two vast islands, Adelaide and Desolation, a passage between the two oceans opens to the west, forming a kind of capital *S*.

But on that day, by a new stroke of misfortune, a violent storm broke, with squalls and gusts of rain, as the wind changed suddenly from west to north.

It was immediately necessary to haul down the light sails, close-reef the topsails, and steer so as to face the waves obliquely and avoid mighty sea swells.

On the night of February thirteenth to fourteenth, there was not a moment of rest. The captain and officers couldn't leave their stations. During the day of the thirteenth, the sky's condition had not permitted calculations, but they estimated that the clipper must be broadside of the straits.

However, entering them in bad weather was very difficult and required extreme caution, as a ship that missed its mark could run aground. It might have been better to return to the west and confront the high seas, while waiting for the storm to blow over and normal winds to return.

If a lighthouse had permitted to precisely gauge the bearing of Cape Pilares, perhaps *The Jonathan* would have entered the straits, since there was a thirty-kilometer opening between this cape and Cape Parker. But Cape Pilares, like Cape Horn, had no lighthouse. This part of the seacoast was not illuminated, and as stated before, there were no lighthouses on the Atlantic before Terre des Etats.

There was no doubt that *The Jonathan* had arrived at the straits' opening, but she would have broken up against the Cape Pilares rocks without a strict watch on board, with attention paid by lookouts fore and aft. Amid the gloom, its vast confused mass was seen just in time, and they swerved quickly enough so as not to fly into the coastline.

Truly, in these conditions, with the violent northern wind and the sea with contrary currents, the turning ship might have run aground. When the rudder's action finally worked, the clipper's stem was only a half-cable's length from the reef. It was necessary to wear, and quickly raise a storm sail on the mizzenmast.

With the tacking finished, *The Jonathan* headed away from this trap to the open sea.

A few hours after dawn, Captain Leccar measured their position. He gauged land at seven or eight miles to the east, but Cape Pilares was already far behind. The storm was at full force, with no signs of calming. With sails lowered, *The Jonathan* was unable to face the northern wind. The ship might have been in distress, had she fought against the squall that showered her with large breaking waves.

Captain Leccar had to change his plans. The clipper was carried away to the south by the ever-augmenting violent wind, beyond Otway Bay, and was in danger of breaking up against the Week Islets. After passing Cape Tate on the Tierra del Desolation, it was impossible to return up toward Cape Pilares. Therefore, they had to give up going by the straits, and instead sailed down south to reach the Atlantic by way of Cape Horn.

After a discussion on this subject between the captain and his officers, the order was given to turn to the open sea and full-reef the topsails, at the speed of the quartering wind. Indeed, sailboats were not accustomed to go alongside this series of islands and islets, against which the sea broke violently, and which contained hundreds of reefs. It was better to approach the Magellanic waters at the latitude of the fifty-sixth parallel south, and follow it while keeping the cape to portside, and the Diego Ramirez Islets to starboard. Perhaps *The Jonathan* would meet more favorable winds on the surface of the Atlantic, which would bring it back to the Cape of Good Hope.

But it was a misfortune to leave the route of the straits, both shorter and comparatively easy for sailboats going from west to east. Captain Leccar had contemplated going back there without returning to look for Cape Pilares. A pilot experienced with the archipelago, like Karroly, might have successfully taken the Cockburn Canal to the south of Tierra del Desolation, gone around Clarence Island, either at its northwest or southeast edges, in order to reach Cape Froward—which juts out a third of the way from the Brunswick Peninsula into the straits—while avoiding the high seas. From there, *The Jonathan* could have returned to the north, passing by Port Famine, Punta Arenas, and after crossing the two channels, disembogued between the Cape des Vierges and Cape Espiritu-Santo on the Atlantic, almost at the latitude of the fifty-second parallel. This plan could certainly have been followed. But without a pilot who knew the coast, it would have been imprudent to venture into a maze of islets and islands, and Captain Leccar was right to recuse even though he could locate them on the precise maps of these waters.

The Jonathan continued to descend southeast as far as the sea's condition permitted, at more than thirty miles from Stewart, Gilbert, and Londonderry Islands. On the afternoon of the fifteenth, after twenty-four hours of difficult sailing, they were broadside on to the Santo Ildefonso Islets.

Unfortunately, the violent storm had not yet calmed. The open space where the waters of the Atlantic and Pacific collide offered the two oceans free course for combat. Captain Leccar must have regretted even more having missed the straits' entrance, where he would have found many places to put into port.

It was the beginning of evening. The wind blew wildly. The

sea, cruel and rough, was placing frightful stress on the vessel, which could not support its ever-more reduced sails.

The night of February fifteenth to sixteenth was horrible. From both sides of America, sidelong squalls ran and collided in the Cape Horn waters, where the clipper struggled against the two oceans' buffets.

Around six o'clock, the squalls were such that *The Jonathan*'s two mizzenmasts snapped and fell over the handrails. An error at the tiller, which could not be avoided, knocked over several men, putting the vessel on its side in the waves. She heeled over to starboard and almost ran aground. It was feared that she would not right herself, for vast amounts of water flooded her bridge, and the scupperholes did not offer her enough outlet. However, they managed to right her, and the topsail, quickly counterbraced on the orders of Lieutenant Furner, was uprighted again in the squall.

But Captain Leccar had been swept away by a wave, and it was impossible to save him. Two sailors were carried overboard with him; the first mate Musgrave and Lieutenant Maddison, mortally wounded in the mizzenmasts' fall, were further victims of the swell.

Such was the situation. A disabled vessel, her captain dead, the first mate and lieutenant who wouldn't survive their injuries, and a crew diminished by several sailors! The sole remaining commanders were a twenty-three-year-old officer, Lieutenant Furster, Petty Officer First Class Tom Sand, two petty officers second class, and as ship's crew, only seventeen men!

As for the passengers, who had refused to stay in the steerage or inside the deckhouses, several also died, and it was impossible to maintain order among the panicked mob.

Around seven o'clock a sudden calm occurred, and although the sea did not fall off, at least the north winds dropped abruptly, as if all air had been removed from the space. A few minutes later, the gusts began again, stronger than before, and this time were hurled from the south against the indestructible masses of the American archipelago.

The vessel was clearly in a desperate situation, deprived of its aft masting, which made it impossible to hoist sails and follow the cape, to battle the new storm sent from faraway Antarctic regions. Moreover, the squall from the north crossed the one from the south, with a sudden change of wind that made the sea rage. It seemed that the already deep gloom grew darker with the violent storm.

Now that the vessel ran toward land and it was humanly impossible to change course, how far away was the land where shipwreck awaited? Lieutenant Furner and the boatswain Tom Land estimated it was less than ten miles away. The land had to be Magellania, whose channels and islands offered places to put in, but *The Jonathan* would be wrecked against it before being able to find shelter there.

They tried at least to delay the final disaster until daybreak. Then the shipwreck would have at least a few chances for rescue. The lieutenant and petty officers first class fixed the vessel under bare poles, by lowering the two topsails, which were the only remaining sails. But the weight of this wide four-master gave the wind enough prize so that it moved at a considerable speed, augmented by the squall. The collision would surely occur in the middle of the night, when *The Jonathan* would smash against the Cape Horn rocks.

Although no one knew what help could be expected or where it would come from, the cannon fired a danger signal amid the frightful tumult of wind and sea. The thick darkness was shattered by the explosive bursts that did not echo at this distance from land.

The Jonathan drifted toward the coastline.

As we know, when the vessel was a few miles from land, where a fire was lit at the top of the foreland, Kaw-djer, just when he was about to commit suicide, risked death in order to save hundreds of people in danger, as Karroly's longboat advanced toward the ship in distress and at risk of sinking countless times amid the breaking squall.

As we know, the *Wel-kiej* came alongside the clipper, the Indian and his son made it fast to the tackle hanging from the aft, and the two men and boy leapt onto the deck that was mobbed by a terrified crowd, while the crew had been decimated, with the captain dead, and two main officers mortally wounded.

As we know, following Kaw-djer's orders, Karroly grabbed the tiller and risked everything, sending the clipper across the Hermitte Island Channel, after leaving the cape on the starboard side.

Finally, as we know, the catastrophe could not be avoided and under the circumstances, as *The Jonathan* drifted north, sheltered from the heights of Horn Island, encountered the stormy sea at the end of the channel, set a storm jib on the foremast to keep on course for the Hermitte Island moorage—the fall of the mainmast and foremast costing more lives, the clipper losing its last sail, exposed to the full rage of wind and sea—and ran aground at the tip of Hoste Island, called False Cape Horn.

It was three o'clock in the morning, and the first signs of dawn had not yet pierced through the sky's deep gloom.

After hitting the rocks of the island, *The Jonathan* turned over halfway on its starboard side, and from her torn hull there came cracks that were louder than the storm's noise.

No sooner had they collided than the unfortunate castaways panicked. Some went overboard, either voluntarily or thrown over by the impact, and fell upon the reefs where the undertow rolled them like flotsam, mutilated and lifeless.

After the shock, *The Jonathan* remained still. She had been upended at high tide, and the ebb tide started to draw the squall toward the east.

Kaw-djer, Lieutenant Furner, and the boatswain Tom Land, managed with some difficulty to restore order among the emigrants, who were finally reassured by the boat's stillness, and there was nothing left to do but wait for the sunrise.

X

HOSTE ISLAND

Hoste Island is one of the middle points of the Magellanic Archipelago. Its northern coastline, which nearly follows the direction of the fifty-fifth parallel, borders the Beagle Canal over half of its length. Its shore is noticeably rectilinear to the north, but is highly irregular on the other coasts of the perimeter. A right angle marks its western border, at the entrance to Darwin Sound, separating it from Gordon Island. Below is a narrow bay at the end of Rous Promontory, in front of which the reefs of Waterman Island endlessly foam. There the coastline recedes, bristling with headlands, protected from the high seas by a belt of islets, Wood, Hope, and Henderson. A deep indentation of the eastern shore intersects Nassau Bay, which opens between Navarin and Wollaston Islands, and Hardy Peninsula projects to the southeast, curved like a scimitar, with False Cape Horn as its narrowed point.

Inside this peninsula, on the other side of an enormous granite mass, *The Jonathan* ran aground obliquely on the coast, with its fore on the beach and aft in the water.

According to maps drawn by King and Fitzroy, Hoste Island is approximately twenty-five leagues long, following Beagle Canal's shoreline. Its maximum width is ten leagues from north to south. These measurements do not include Hardy Peninsula, which is already narrow where it begins, and whose curves extend for about a dozen leagues.

The short and jagged peninsula's outlines appeared in the mists of dawn, which sped away the last bit of the storm's fury.

A perpendicular hillock near the sea made a sharp crest with the foreland, forming an acute watershed with the peninsula's form. A bed of blackish rocks spread beneath the hillock, mostly covered at high tide but now visible at low tide, covered with slimy wrack and kelp. A few slabs of white sand made large white spots between the reefs, a smooth and still-wet sand, richly spangled with the shells, terebratulae, fissurellas, limpets, tritons, sea unicorns, chitons, surf clams, and venuses, which abounded on Magellanic beaches.

Nothing kept the passengers on the vessel's deck. Naturally, they were eager to regain dry land, even though their vessel, lying on the rocks, had left its natural element.

For a moment, they were shaken by warping at the stem, and around one hundred people advanced northwest into the peninsula. Others, impatient to reconnoiter their position, tried to scale the foreland's steep slopes, whose height of around two hundred feet allowed them to see a portion of the island.

Kaw-djer and Karroly asked Lieutenant Furner and the boatswain to follow them, in order to examine the site of *The Jonathan*'s shipwreck. It was worth knowing if the rising sea would set them afloat again, or if she was forever lost.

One of the passengers joined them, Mr. Harry Rhodes, whose wife, son, and daughter remained aboard, a man about fifty years old who ranked highly among the emigrants.

Kaw-djer had tried in vain, it must be added, to save the injured first mate, Musgrave, and Lieutenant Maddison, whose bodies were in their cabins. Among the clipper's officers, John Furner was the sole survivor.

The passengers did not have a good first impression of the land. False Cape Horn was uniquely dismal. If its aridity continued farther off, the castaways would not find enough to eat, once *The Jonathan*'s food stores ran out. And in one month, the stormy season would begin, early as usual Magellania, and if luck did not bring another vessel to these waters, if no help came from Punta Arenas, they would be doomed to an arduous winter on the Hoste Island coastline.

Kaw-djer, Lieutenant Furner, Tom Land, and Mr. Harry Rhodes first discussed this subject. The lieutenant's first question was:

"*The Jonathan* was wrecked in what part of Magellania?"

"Hoste Island," replied Kaw-djer.

"On the Magellan Straits?" asked Mr. Rhodes.

"No, on Beagle Canal that separates it from Tierra del Fuego."

"Which we should not be too far from," said the boatswain, "and which we could have reached with our small boats, if they hadn't been swept away . . ."

"In any case, we still have the longboat that you brought aboard," Lieutenant Furner remarked to Kaw-djer.

"Is it in good shape?" asked Mr. Rhodes.

"In good shape," replied Karroly, whose first concern had been to visit the *Wel-kiej*, where his son stayed with the dog Zol.

"One longboat to carry several hundred passengers," said Kaw-djer, "means a long, arduous, and perhaps dangerous trip, if the bad weather continues . . . And then . . . to abandon the cargo . . . foodstuffs . . . equipment . . .?"

Of course this conversation was in English, a language that Karroly understood and spoke in his piloting jobs. To this suggestion of leaving the island, he broke in, saying:

"What use is looking for shelter on Tierra del Fuego? Hoste Island offers the same resources . . . *The Jonathan*'s castaways can certainly spend the winter here."

"That's what I think," said Kaw-djer, " and it's the advice I'd give . . ."

While Karroly spoke, Mr. Rhodes watched him attentively and realized that he was an Indian.

"Who are you?" he asked, just as Lieutenant Furner was about to ask the same question.

"The pilot Karroly."

"Well, pilot, I thank you on behalf of the passengers and crew. You risked your life to save us, and even though our ship is a wreck, many people owe their lives to you."

Then he said to Kaw-djer:

"And you, sir, who are . . .?"

"No matter," said Kaw-djer.

"A fellow countryman perhaps?"

"A friend of the Fuegians . . . in Magellania for several years," declared Kaw-djer.

Mr. Rhodes did not insist. Doubtless he understood that a secret had to be kept. But he was obliged to express gratitude for the two men's devotion. Without their actions, if Kaw-djer had not thought to signal from shore by lighting the top of the foreland, and had he not given the order to send the longboat into the squall, if Karroly had not taken the drifting ship's rudder in hand, had he lacked the boldness and skill to guide it toward the channel to reach the island's shelter, *The Jonathan* would have smashed against the rocks of Horn Island, and no one would have survived the wreck. Indeed, the ship's putting in on the coast of Hoste Island's foreland was the result of a final accident, which removed control of the ship from the pilot.

There were already too many victims: the captain, the first mate, the lieutenant, a dozen sailors, and as many passengers. But they would have numbered in the hundreds at the foot of Cape Horn!

However, since the tide was low, the lieutenant and his companions climbed down the hillock to inspect the vessel's hull, which was almost entirely exposed on the rocks. On the beach Mr. Rhodes rejoined his wife and children. Kaw-djer, perhaps wishing to keep apart, went to the peninsula's point.

It was quickly seen that *The Jonathan* was definitively wrecked. The hull was smashed in twenty places, ripped up along almost the entire starboard side. This was permanent damage for an iron ship, whereas a wooden ship can be refloated. They had to abandon all hope of relaunching it, and the sea would soon complete its destruction.

"What we must do, without losing a single day," said Tom Land, "is save the cargo, and put it in a safe place. When the tide rises, the sea will penetrate inside the hold, and the provisions we need will be damaged."

"Not only the provisions," said Lieutenant Furner, "but the equipment as well. Who knows, we may have to spend the winter on this island, through the bad weather, until we can get back home."

"Everybody get to work!" said the boatswain.

Indeed, the most urgent task was to unload *The Jonathan*, which would be destroyed by the next storm, and make it possible to stay for a few months on the island without any contact from Chile or Argentina. There was no transportation available for reaching Punta Arenas. But they would take care to alert the Chilean authorities, in order to be sent a means of getting home when spring returned.

The Lieutenant and the boatswain gave orders for the vessel's unloading. Germans, Americans, and Irishmen understood the urgency of the task and went at it with courage and energy. As we know, the ship's hold contained considerable equipment for establishing the new colony, not only tents but also some houses and stores, whose different parts were easily assembled and used. Manpower was not lacking for this task, which was completed in short order. Meanwhile, news of the shipwreck spread through Magellania. Fuegians and Pecherais began to arrive from islands neighboring Hoste Island and Tierra del Fuego. Motivated by the lure of profit, they offered their services, which were naturally accepted. There was nothing to fear from these gentle and peaceful natives, unlike the thieving and warlike Patagonians, whose participation was not missed.

As winter began, the work was finished in an organized way. Lieutenant Furner maintained shipboard discipline for the castaways, helped by Mr. Rhodes and other emigrants who had some influence over their companions. It would be unfortunate if disorder reigned over these people of different nationalities, if they refused to recognize any authority.

Mr. Rhodes and the colonists who followed his orders were afraid of this, with some cause. They recalled what had happened during the Pacific crossing, the rebellious ideas propagated among a number of passengers, the brothers John and Jack Merritt's disastrous meddling and the influence they had acquired over some of their companions. They recalled how the late Captain Leccar was obliged to act against these fomenters of revolution, and several times had forbidden them any contact with the passengers. Would they take advantage of the situation to start agitating again, and provoke a rebellion at a time when the fullest accord was needed for the common good?

At first, the Merritt brothers behaved normally, knowing that they were being closely watched. At any rate, they were free to leave the wintering station and take their supporters to some other part of the island, after having claimed part of the cargo. They did not do so, instead joining the other passengers who, following orders from the Lieutenant, were unloading the vessel. And what would the future bring—would they take up their loathsome propaganda again during the long months of isolation?

Of course, there was no question of founding a colony on the Hoste Island coastline. The emigrants had not reached their destination, but were mere castaways who could not return home for several months, and whose only care was to survive the winter.

Moreover, they were not in the far graver situation of castaways who are thrown onto a land whose name and bearings are unknown, one of those isolated islands of the Pacific Ocean, out of reach of any contact with ships.

No, the disaster occurred on the Magellanic Archipelago, on the Hardy peninsula of Hoste Island, which is precisely mapped, and well known to Kaw-djer and the pilot Karroly, in the portion of the archipelago which now belonged to the Chilean government, at most about one hundred leagues from Punta Arenas, the capital of Chilean Magellania. News of the shipwreck would shortly be well known there, and as soon as weather permitted, a ship would be sent, whether from the ports of southern America or from the same port in San Francisco, California, from which *The Jonathan* left some weeks before.

Therefore there were no serious problems to expect, once acceptable housing was built on Hoste Island. The equipment provided shelter, and the cargo provided food. Were it not for the difficult climate that they had to endure, the emigrants could live there as they would have lived during the first months of their stay on African soil.

Three weeks after the shipwreck—the unloading was completed in about a week—a campground was organized on the Hardy Peninsula on March 17, and allowed them to await the arrival of winter without too much concern.

Meanwhile, explorations were made to all regions around the campground. The Hardy Peninsula looked forlorn up to the dry extremities of False Cape Horn, but this was not true of the green region whose peaks were outlined to the northwest. After rocks covered with wrack, and ravines bristling with shrubs, came vast prairies, virgin pasture ground that bordered wooded hills, at the foot of which grew sentry box flowers framing the peninsula. They were mixed with yellow-flowered leopard's bane, blue-and-violet flowered sea asters, groundsels with meter-length stems, and many dwarf plants like slipperwort, creeping laburnum, large-fruited ancistres, brome grass, feather grass, and tiny bloodwort in full flower. Pasture followed pasture, softened by luxurious grass, where hundreds of ruminants might have pastured. Indeed, the ovine and bovine breeds that had embarked aboard *The Jonathan* were up to their bellies in the thick grasses.

One of these trips led Mr. Rhodes and some of the colonists a dozen miles to the northwest. They were accompanied by Kawdjer, who serviceably acted as guide. They visited Bourchier Bay on the west coast of the peninsula, Orange and Scotchwell Bays, and farther on, the peninsula that would later be named after Pasteur, between Tekinika Sound and Posonby Sound, whose mountains are perpetually snow-covered.

Their wonderment equaled their surprise. The rich pastures everywhere proved the soil's fertility, irrigated by a network of little creeks, which flowed into a small river with bright, limpid water that originated in the central hills. The tree growth matched the luxurious tapestry on the plains. The forests, framing vast spaces, were made up specifically of superbly sturdy antarctic beeches, rooted in peaty but rich soil, and offering an open undergrowth, sometimes covered with branching moss. There were birchwood and drimys of two meters' circumference at their bases. There were winter bark trees, and barberries, a sort of sorrel thornbush whose wood is extraordinarily solid, and species of conifers resembling cypresses, from thirty to forty feet high.

A world of flying animals sported under these green vaults, six species of tinamous, some as big as pebbles and others like pheasants, thrushes, and blackbirds, which might be called country birds, and also a variety of aquatic species, like geese, ducks, cormorants and seagulls. Leaping across the prairies were nandu ostriches, guanacos, and vicunas.

The castaways set up their temporary campground half a mile away from the spot where *The Jonathan* was wrecked, in the center of the curve formed by Hardy Peninsula, which joins the high ground to the west. A river appeared there with shaded banks, enlarged by its many sources, whose water flowed to the sea from the back of a small cove. Its banks, one hundred feet apart, would have been an easy place to build a village for permanent lodging. If need be, the cove could serve as a port, being sheltered from high winds by the large hillock, nearly six hundred meters tall.

Kaw-djer and Karroly had advised the emigrants to camp there for the winter. There was room for their housing equipment there. Moreover, they asserted, the bad weather, between April and October, was not as fearsome as Magellania's position above the fifty-second parallel might lead them to believe. The climate spared them the excessive rigors of the polar regions, and under the blanket of snow that covered it for several months of the year, the cold was never unbearable.

Surely, misfortune had cruelly tested *The Jonathan*'s passengers. When they should have been in the middle of the Atlantic, sailing toward the Cape of Good Hope, they were instead forced to stay for a certain time on an island in the Magellanic Archipelago. But they would be free after a few months' delay and would only have lost the shipwreck victims.

Mr. Rhodes frequently spoke about such things with Kaw-djer. Mrs. Rhodes, a serious and sensible woman, her eighteen-year-old son, Edward, and her fifteen-year-old daughter, Clary, felt attracted to this man, as did Mr. Rhodes, although they could not explain his solitary life among the remote archipelago's Indians. For his part, Kaw-djer seemed to feel a certain sympathy for this family, whose qualities and virtues were recognized by many other colonists. Surely in the new colony, Mr. Rhodes would be called upon to exert a healthy influence, and the best people would always be on his side.

However, Kaw-djer did not unburden himself and invariably maintained his usual reticence. He offered his advice to everyone, which were followed during the moving-in work. Only the Merritt brothers and a few others did not seek him out, unaware that he was, like themselves, an enemy of all social organizations. Since what might be called Kaw-djer's return to life in order to accomplish a humane act, did he still think about his projects? And if he absolutely did not wish to remain on this land that had become Chilean, would he head off once again to Cape Horn?

The Yacana campground—as this waterside area on Hoste Island was called—included tents and some houses assembled after the cargo had been stored. The vessel had to be abandoned, and it was demolished more with each rising tide. Houses and tents had been set up on the left bank of the Yacana River, and a half mile farther down the same bank were pasture grounds that covered the island's eastern portion. Storehouses, set up under the shelter of tall beeches, contained reserves of provisions, grains, preserved meats, food—everything that would be useful for starting the colony at the Orange River's mouth. Farmyards had been organized for poultry, and sties for pigs. Cows, goats, and sheep were placed in enclosures in neighboring pastures.

Understandably, strict disciple was needed for nearly a thousand emigrants of diverse origins sharing a life together. The young lieutenant was not the man to impose an efficient authority. Had Captain Leccar or even the first mate Musgrave been there, perhaps they might have been able to maintain order among the castaways, as they had for the passengers. But they were dead, and on the island no one seemed capable of commanding the rest. Moreover, there was always the fear that the Merritt brothers might provoke bad sentiments, sowing discord when it was so important for everyone to get along!

Soon, the Chilean government would want to intervene. The island belonged to them, and the castaways would obviously approach them to be repatriated. It was decided that Karroly and his son would go to Punta Arenas to apprise His Excellency Mr. Aguire of the situation.

As it seemed suitable that one of the emigrants accompany the pilot, Mr. Rhodes offered to travel aboard the *Wel-kiej*. The American would be more qualified than the Indian Karroly for the procedures needed to win the government's cooperation. At first, John and Jack Merritt were opposed to the project, which would put the emigrants under Chilean authority, but finally they were obliged to give in. Kaw-djer, who was consulted for the common good, approved the decision, but had already decided to leave Hoste Island himself before the representatives from Punta Arenas arrived.

Having bid farewell to his family and companions, Mr. Rhodes embarked on the morning of March twentieth, and after Karroly turned around the tip of the Hardy Peninsula, he crossed Nassau Bay in order to follow the narrow Mugray Channel between Hoste and Navarin Islands. After emerging in Beagle Canal, he went up west as far as Clarence Island, and reached the Magellan Straits almost facing Cape Froward.

It was calculated that the longboat should return in three weeks, or before winter would make the *Wel-kiej*'s sailing across the archipelago's sound difficult or impossible.

During this time, communal life took shape, as it would have in the new colony of Orange River. Apart from the Merritt brothers and some of their supporters who chose to live separately, there were no hitches.

On the afternoon of April ninth, the longboat was seen in the waters around the tip, and as soon as it had docked, Mr. Rhodes debarked at the place where his family and friends awaited him.

After arriving at Punta Arenas, Mr. Rhodes had visited Mr. Aguire, who was already informed about wreck of *The Jonathan*. The Chilean government, thus advised, would take measures to repatriate the emigrants. But there was no vessel in Punta Arenas that could be assigned to carry the castaways to Valparaiso or another South American port. For the moment, the situation wasn't worrisome, with camping equipment in good condition and enough foodstuffs for a whole year. The best thing would be to resign themselves to a few months' stay on Hoste Island. The governor would keep an eye on them. A sloop stationed at Punta Arenas would soon be sent to the island, and maintain order there if needed.

Such was the response brought back by Mr. Rhodes. The colonists could count on the Chilean government's good will to ensure them a calm stay while they awaited repatriation. The winter season that would soon cover the Magellanic Archipelago with snow could be anticipated without excessive concern.

XI

WINTERING

Winter began in the first weeks of April with substantial atmospheric disturbances; but the storms did not catch *The Jonathan*'s passengers unprepared, as the temporary colonists were settled enough on Hoste Island not to suffer from wind or cold. Most lived in watertight huts. Equipped with stoves fed by the abundant firewood from nearby forests, they could weather the drop in temperature, which was only slight in Magellania.

Until then, a certain number of emigrants—at most one hundred—had preferred to remain in *The Jonathan*'s deckhouses or galleys, even though the ship's listing made life aboard uncomfortable. But two or three gusts of wind from the south raised the sea across the channels and smashed into the Hardy Peninsula. The clipper's hull, already much damaged, opened bit by bit, and its total destruction was only a matter of time. It was therefore imprudent to remain aboard, and the families had to move to the remaining tents, where they were better off than the Fuegians in their ajoupas and wigwams. *The Jonathan* soon became a shapeless shell, emptied of everything usable.

The longboat was safely located at the back of a rock basin near the Yacana River's mouth; it felt nothing of the open sea squall, which broke on the reefs. Kaw-djer, Karroly, and Halg remained aboard, waiting to depart, although no date had been set.

After the strong southwestern winds, the atmospheric disturbances stopped. The improvised village did not suffer too much, and neither huts nor tents were threatened by the worst of the storm, because of their location on the river's left bank, on the other side of a sheltering bluff. Then the temperature lowered and the first harsh cold of winter was felt.

To answer some concerns that were expressed, Kaw-djer reassured the emigrant group. Magellania's average temperature of less than zero centigrade [thirty-two degrees Fahrenheit] made winter easier and shorter than in Ireland, Canada, or the northern United States insofar as the American, Canadian, and Irish emigrants were concerned. The archipelago's climate was akin to that of subequatorial Africa.

This was a frequent subject of conversation for Mr. Rhodes' family. The family got closer and closer to Kaw-djer and felt they would indeed be sorry when the day came to separate.

It must be repeated that Mr. Rhodes was a highly educated and sensible man, whose deep religious beliefs were shared by his entire family. He had lived in Madison, Wisconsin, until unpredictable business reversals ruined him. Whence the project to expatriate to an African colony to make a fortune—more for the sake of his children than for himself. Mrs. Rhodes, a strong and serious woman, encouraged his plan and was ready to second him in a hard-working emigrant's life. Soon they left Madison for good, accompanied by their two beloved children who loved them in return. One could say that this family had won the community's sympathy, and their influence in the future colony could only grow with time.

Mr. Rhodes' hut was built on the Yacana River's right bank, near two dozen others around a small square bordered on one side by the riverbank. Beech trees and silver birches shaded this village center. The home was made of four planks for walls, like all those that the colonization company put at the disposal of emigrants, who were responsible for making them more comfortable, and even then, comfort was limited to a few pieces of furniture, bedding, and household utensils.

Kaw-djer spent all his time in this modest dwelling when he was not on trips with Mr. Rhodes and others to different parts of the island. When night fell, he returned to the longboat where Karroly and his son waited, ever-ready to take to the sea again.

Take to the sea? In what direction? Would the *Wel-kiej* return to New Island, which Kaw-djer had seemingly left forever, and we know the deadly ideas he was haunted by when the longboat took him toward Cape Horn. However, he often spoke to the inhabitants about leaving soon.

One day Mr. Rhodes asked him:

"Why do you want to leave us, now that you've become our friend? Why not stay here during the wintering?"

Kaw-djer did not reply.

Mrs. Rhodes added, "When a ship will come for us at Hoste Island, won't it seem all too soon for us to separate, with the sad thought that we'll never meet again?"

Young Marc added [Verne changed Edward Rhodes' name to Marc in mid-story], "You saved us!"

Clary Rhodes pleaded, "Oh! Stay, Mr. Kaw-djer!"

Kaw-djer shook his head like a man whose mind was made up.

He said, "I can't...and I must leave soon . . . Yes, very soon!"

"To return to New Island?" asked Mr. Rhodes. "What'll you do there that you can't do here—hunt, fish, and traffic your skins? What keeps you from spending the whole winter with us?"

Thus pressed, Kaw-djer dodged questions, not replying, at least about himself. He fell back on Karroly as an excuse. The Indian and his son could not abandon their home on New Island. They had definitively fixed their house there, where Kaw-djer came to share their solitary existence. Karroly was best situated there his pilot's work, and captains called him by raising a white banner with blue piping, when they were ready to go up toward Beagle Canal. If Karroly was no longer at his post on New Island, the vessels would head for the archipelago's other channels.

Mr. Rhodes, stubbornly refusing to give up, said, "But ships hardly ever come to these waters in the winter, and there is no piloting to do between March and October . . . One might say that coastal trading is suspended for at least five months. The end of March would be the time to return to New Island."

Kaw-djer kept quiet, and his hosts felt that they had touched upon the mystery of this man's life.

"Anyway," added Mr. Rhodes, "why shouldn't the Indian go alone with his son?"

Kaw-djer replied, "No. I would not agree to separate from him. We have lived together for many years, and it would cause him as much pain as it would cause me . . ."

"Let him stay then, my friend," Mrs. Rhodes insisted, "but don't think of leaving. See how your presence is useful for us, and what would become of us if you left? There are many women and children here to doctor, and you are the only one who can provide this care! Winter is upon us, and who knows, it may be severe . . ."

"Severe? No, Mrs. Rhodes, don't worry about any such thing. I am experienced in this land, and I repeat, even in July, the middle of winter, the cold is bearable. In America, the northern wind comes from the icy polar regions. Here the southern winds cross vast seas that don't chill them."

The Rhodes family often chatted in this manner, adding their prayers to those from other families who had many reasons to insist on Kaw-djer's presence during the wintering. They saw him as devoted, humane, and capable of doctoring people. He had at his disposal all the pharmaceutical goods from the shipwrecked vessel, and what fine use he made of them!

Yes, it would have been a humane act to remain on Hoste Island. Kaw-djer felt this, and perhaps a struggle was going on inside him. But those who wanted to hold onto him could not imagine that he expected, from day to day, the Punta Arenas governor's representatives to arrive. He knew how suspicious his presence in Magellania seemed. If he were discovered among *The Jonathan's* castaways, he would be interrogated, just as they had hoped to do on New Island. In order not to reveal his identity, he had already once fled the Magellanic territory whose independence had been destroyed by the 1881 treaty.

But he did not leave, and it soon became time for the Punta Arenas sloop to hove into view of Hoste Island, or even for the ship sent to repatriate *The Jonathan*'s castaways to arrive.

Each morning he climbed to the top of the bluff, and neither Mr. Rhodes nor anyone else could guess why he looked so stubbornly out to the open sea.

Now, it became improbable that a ship would cross the archipelago's channels. Snowstorms sometimes swept across them with remarkable violence, and thrusting ice soon made them unnavigable.

The month of May was ending, and the cold was not yet severe, which confirmed Kaw-djer's statements. As he no longer spoke of his departure, Mr. and Mrs. Rhodes did not raise the subject again. He was still there, that's what mattered. Every morning, the longboat was seen at its berth. Kaw-djer continued to give medical care to all those who asked for it, a benefactor to the castaways, as he had been to the natives.

It is only fair to add that not only his care, but also the advice from a man who knew the region, its climate and resources, was of great service to those wintering on Hoste Island.

The winter's short days and long nights went by, and, most importantly, health conditions in this little world did not break down. A few acute illnesses occurred, easily cured by Kaw-djer, and there were a few deaths of young children who might not have survived in the southern African climate either.

It was fortunate that *The Jonathan*'s castaways had not been thrown onto Hoste Island in the middle of the winter season. How different their impressions would have been! Instead of verdant plains, forests bursting with summer foliage, and a mostly sunny sky, there would have been grayish mist hiding the hilltops, clumps of trees crusted with hoarfrost, leaves hanging down like silvery tongues, an immense tapestry of snow that obliterating the bluff, the shore, and the Yacana River's banks; all the tents, shops, and huts would have felt like a village at the back of the Siberian Steppes.

An even sadder impression would have struck the castaways if *The Jonathan* had been wrecked on the Clarence, Desolation, or William territories where Pacific storms rage on the western part of the archipelago, even on the long peninsula of Mount Sarmiento at the end of Tierra del Fuego, which in this season became a Land of Ice! There the mountains are higher and their peaks never shake off the fog that bathes them, even under the summer sun. On the different levels of the orographic system, the brilliant gleam of glaciers is permanent. There is an indescribable chaos of mountains with domes, peaks, and pinnacles, and the prodigious muddle of their branching-out results in the last upthrust of the Andean cordillera, which peters out at the new continent's tip.

Such were the differences presented by the two halves of the Magellanic Archipelago. Nature had favored the western one—of Tierra del Fuego and the islands near it. The treaty of 1881 had been fairly negotiated by the two disputing powers. Why was it necessary for the agreement to cost the region its independence?

It should be observed that animal life was never scarce, even when the archipelago suffered the winter season's harshness, when storms hit with extreme violence, when the heights were topped with ice and the soil vanished under the snow. The forest still sheltered large numbers of ruminants, ostriches, guanacos, vicunas, and foxes. Across the prairies flew mountain geese, small partridges, woodcocks, and snipe. The seacoast pullulated with edible larks, large sea birds, albatrosses, and oyster catchers with yellow feet and red beaks. Whales came to blow right up to the neighboring channels, and sea lions were abundant on the beaches. Between the rocks, amid algae were hake, lamprey, large shellfish, and even small-sized Galaxiidae in the Yacana River's waters.

It followed that hunters and fishermen could be economical with *The Jonathan*'s provisions, while obtaining fresh and healthy food, for as a number of explorers have noted, game from the Fuegian region and Patagonia is of superior quality.

Around fifty of the Irish and Americans spent their spare time fruitfully as sea lion hunters under Karroly's direction. As a result, even though Hoste Island was not usually inhabited, it could have been, and could have fed a few thousand dwellers.

The coldest month was July, with dry weather and a clear sky, and the temperature never dropped below seven degrees centigrade [around forty-four degrees Fahrenheit]. Some ice festooned the beaches, and upstream the Yacana River froze enough to make it possible to walk from one bank to the other. Needless to say, the large thoroughfare that separated the Patagonian and Magellanic territories never froze over, and vessels could always cross it. They were present in Beagle Canal and the straits, and the port at Hardy Peninsula never closed, any more than did the port at Punta Arenas.

During the winter season, Hoste Island was always visited by some natives. Fuegians came to fish in Nassau Bay and stayed for several weeks on the northern side of Hardy Peninsula.

The emigrants were pleased by their contacts with the Pecherais, as cordial as they had been with the Indians who worked to unload the cargo. Kaw-djer found his Fuegian patients among them, and the affection and adoration they showed him was expressed in their eagerness and signs of gratitude. One day, Mr. Rhodes could not hide how touched he was by the impoverished natives' behavior.

"I can understand," he said, "that you are attached to a country where you do such humane work, and you are in a hurry to return to these tribes. You are a God for them . . ."

"A God!" replied Kaw-djer. "Why a God, when it's enough to be a man in order to do good?"

Mr. Rhodes, with all his fervent belief in a good and just God, was saddened to find Kaw-djer an atheist and materialist, and he never raised the subject again. All he did was reply:

"Be that as it may, since the name offends you; but you might have been King of Magellania in the days when it was independent."

"Men, even if they are only savages," said Kaw-djer, "have no more need of a God than a master, and besides, the Fuegians have a master now . . . and I will abandon them . . . I will abandon this country . . ." he added, but so quietly that Mr. Rhodes could not hear him.

At the beginning of October, the first signs of the new season appeared. Snow changed to rain that ran across the grass; hill slopes were striped with bands of greenery; antarctic beeches exposed their white-shrouded structures; trees with indeciduous leaves revealed their foliage; new buds pushed out half-open tips; ice drifted downstream on newly unfrozen water; little by little, the Yacana River's mouth was unblocked; heather swayed its faded branches in the breeze; tree trunks were covered with moss and lichens; the sand shone with seashells profusely scattered by the undertow; sea-tangle, once frozen by the cold, moved amid the rocks; wrack and kelp thickened under the reanimated water; with the sun's help, all nature donned spring colors; intense fragrances, with balsamic scents, spread through the air.

Some days there were still squalls when the bluff received the open sea's dreadful onslaughts; but it was clear that the time of massive storms was over, with the approach of spring calm.

That day, in the Rhodes family hut, there was a celebration for the return of spring, as the winterers would certainly be leaving Hoste Island before the season was over.

The sky was clear, the air calm, and the sun shining. The thermometer read nine degrees above zero centigrade. During the morning and afternoon, people walked along the shore at the foot of the hillock, near the Yacana River's banks, to breathe the sea air.

After lunch Kaw-djer accompanied his friends on their walk. They crossed the waterway in *The Jonathan*'s dinghy. From this side, some sea lion hunters could be seen hunting the amphibians who crawled on the beaches and hoisted themselves up onto the sides of rocks, or slept at the foot of the bluff.

Kaw-djer seemed more worried and quieter than usual, no doubt about the idea that the day approached when he must leave this honorable family whose affectionate contact had reawakened in him social instincts that are so natural to man. He felt grief over admitting that he would never see this honest and good friend, who was thrown into his path by a shipwreck, as well as his devoted and comforting wife whose qualities he appreciated, and their two children, Marc and Clary, to whom he was so attached! The Rhodes family shared his grief. They all hoped that Kaw-djer would agree to follow them to the African colony, where he would be appreciated, honored, and loved as he was at Hoste Island. But though Mr. Rhodes understood that such a man must have had serious motives for breaking off with humanity, the key to this strange and mysterious life still escaped him.

"Winter is over," said Mrs. Rhodes, "and it really wasn't too harsh . . ."

"And we note," Mr. Rhodes said to Kaw-djer,"that this region's climate is just as our friend told us! More than one of us will somehow regret leaving Hoste Island . . ."

"Well then, let's not leave!" shouted young Marc, "Let's establish a colony in the Magellanic territory!"

"Fine!" replied Mr. Rhodes, smiling, "and what about our land grant on the Orange River, and the colonization company's commitments, and the Portuguese government's commitments . . ."

"Indeed," said Kaw-djer somewhat ironically, "there are commitments with the Portuguese government and they must be kept. Anyway, here it would be the Chilean government, and one is the same as the other!"

"Yes, six months earlier . . . ," remarked Mr. Rhodes.

"Six months earlier," said Kaw-djer, "you would have landed on free soil, whose independence was stolen by a damned treaty!"

Kaw-djer, with his arms crossed, his head held high, looked to the west, as if he expected to see a sloop appear at the entrance of Darwin Sound.

At this moment, the Merritt brothers passed by—noisy troublemakers followed by thirty of their companions—on their way to the island's interior. They never hid their dislike for the Rhodes family, who were rightly honored in this small world, and for Kaw-djer, whose real importance was undeniable.

"There are some people," said Mr. Rhodes, "I would leave here with no regrets. I feel that nothing good can come from them. They'll cause some trouble in our new colony. They accept no authority, and only dream of disorder, following their hateful doctrines! . . . As if order and authority weren't required by every social entity, every nation large or small, whatever its form of government!"

Kaw-djer did not reply, either because he was so absorbed in his own thoughts that he wasn't listening, or because he didn't want to answer.

However, it is fair to note that since the start of the wintering, around one hundred anarchists lived separately and made no attempt to disturb the peace; they considered life on Hoste Island as only temporary. But if for unforeseen reasons the stay were to be prolonged, if the fine weather ended before they were repatriated, perhaps there would be an outburst or revolt that would need to be suppressed, as it was aboard *The Jonathan*.

But that wasn't probable, and the situation would likely be resolved in a few weeks.

Indeed, even before the Chilean sloop arrived, it was possible that the colonists could leave Hoste Island. Since *The Jonathan*'s shipwreck was known about at Punta Arenas, there was reason to believe that the American colonization company must have been notified. Why shouldn't the company equip a vessel to rescue the colonists from Hoste Island and bring them to the African coast? If not, surely steamers would come from Chilean or Argentinean ports to repatriate them to Valparaiso or Buenos Aires.

But the days went by in this expectation, combined with a certain anxiety. Vegetation reappeared with extraordinary vigor. Never were richer pastures offered to ruminants, which would have provided for herds of thousands. Only a few piles of winter snow remained, shaded from the sun, and these soon melted. Hunters and fishermen were soon fully occupied. The former spread across the plains in pursuit of guanacos, vicunas, and ostriches, not to mention cougars and jaguars, the same species as on Tierra del Fuego; the latter worked on neighboring beaches. Karroly, as an expert sea lion hunter, stocked up on furs to bring to New Island when the *Wel-kiej* brought Kaw-djer back there, assuming that he wished to return.

Finally, the last weeks of October arrived. No ships came into sight of the island, apart from some coasting vessels from the Malvinas, which couldn't be used to repatriate the castaways. The governor of Punta Arenas had still not sent the sloop, despite his formal promise to Mr. Rhodes, when he met him months before in the capital of Chilean Magellania.

The colonists were justifiably concerned by this delay. Certainly, Hoste Island provided for all their needs. The cargo's storehouse was far from exhausted and would last for several more months. But they had not reached their destination, and were unwilling to accept a second wintering, so the question arose as to whether they should send the longboat again to Punta Arenas. Kaw-djer was consulted on this matter, and Mr. Rhodes asked him to send the *Wel-kiej* to Punta Arenas.

Surely this suggestion would annoy Kaw-djer, if he intended to return to New Island, or at least to leave Hoste Island. The longboat's trip would take at least three weeks, and his departure would be delayed for this amount of time. In case the Chilean sloop arrived while the *Wel-kiej* was gone, Kaw-djer would no longer be able to avoid the agents of Chilean authority. He was firmly resolved to do so, although he had said nothing about it to the Rhodes family.

Nevertheless he agreed, despite the trouble that it caused him, and it was decided that the longboat would leave the following day, October sixteenth. Once again, Mr. Rhodes would go along, and this time Lieutenant Furner would join him to ask for immediate repatriation for himself and *The Jonathan*'s crew.

That's where things were when every plan changed on the evening of the sixteenth.

Late that day, Kaw-djer, who had climbed the slopes of the hillock as usual, looked at the section of the sea stretching west of False Cape Horn in the direction of Henderson Island.

The sun went down on the horizon, and a long luminous ray trembled on the water's surface, undulating in wide swells.

Suddenly Kaw-djer looked fixedly at an almost imperceptible point about eight or nine miles away. His face darkened, his eyes flashed, and after making sure he was not making a mistake:

"A ship," he murmured, "and no doubt the Chilean sloop!"

Kaw-djer did not climb down yet; he remained at the top of the bluff until sunset. He was not mistaken: it was indeed the sloop maneuvering in order to put in at Hoste Island.

But night had fallen and there was reason to believe that the sloop would not land on Hardy Peninsula before dawn. How could it risk looking for a moorage in the gloom without a pilot as guide?

Kaw-djer stayed at the bluff's top for a few more moments, his heart heavy and spirit agitated; then he climbed down to the shore.

As soon as he announced the news, there was a general expression of joy. A ship was finally arriving, and even if it wasn't the ship that could repatriate them, at least *The Jonathan*'s castaways would enter into contact with Punta Arenas' governor.

Mr. Rhodes and his family returned to their home, and Kaw-djer followed them as usual. The evening was spent in discussions about the future. The question of repatriation was resolved and Mr. Rhodes would not be obliged to go to Punta Arenas.

He distinctly felt that his guest was sadder than usual on this occasion, but his sadness was respected, and when he left around nine o'clock, he embraced the little boy and girl, and affectionately shook the hands of Mr. and Mrs. Rhodes.

The next day, the longboat had left the back of the small cove, and everyone looked for it in vain in the waters around Hoste Island.

XII

THE NEW COLONY

Mr. Rhodes was one of the first to be informed of the *Welkiej*'s departure. He was probably grieved, as were his family and the entire small group of emigrants who for nine months had appreciated Kaw-djer's devotion. Their benefactor's departure had as much effect on them as the vessel's appearance in Hoste Island's waters.

Kaw-djer had left; the longboat took him away with Karroly and his son . . . Where to? Was he headed for New Island, to go back to his solitary life, his trips among Indian tribes, with no thought of returning? Why should he return to the Hardy Peninsula? Wouldn't the temporary settlement on the Yacana River's banks be abandoned? In a short time, the emigrants must leave, whether brought to Valparaiso or Buenos Aires, or in a steamer sent by the colonization company to the African coast.

Such were the thoughts caused by Kaw-djer's sudden departure. Had it occurred on the day when the colonists left Hoste Island, that would have been understandable; why didn't he wait until that day, and why didn't he tell anyone, not even Mr. Rhodes and his family? There had been so many signs of sincere friendship, the ties of which are not broken so abruptly. It is inexcusable not to allow oneself a last farewell. Finally, why such a rapid departure that looked like he was running away? Had the arrival of the Chilean ship provoked it?

All guesses were possible, given the mystery that surrounded the life of this man.

Finally, around eight o'clock in the morning, the sloop put in at three cables' length from the tip of False Cape Horn, and its captain went aground quickly.

Magellania's western and southern parts having become Chilean after the treaty of January 17, 1881, the government, taking advantage of *The Jonathan*'s shipwreck and the presence of several hundred emigrants on Hoste Island, wanted to begin with a masterful initiative.

Presently, the Argentine republic could claim nothing beyond the territories of Patagonia and Tierra del Fuego accorded them, including the Tierra des Etats beyond the Le Maire Straits; on its own territory, Chile was free to act in its own interest. It was not enough to claim possession of a previously undivided land, where other countries might have laid claims of prior occupation. Taking advantage of it was essential, by exploiting the soil's mineral and agricultural riches, enriching it by labor and trade, bringing settlers there if it were uninhabited: in short, to colonize it. Following the example that had been set on the western coast of the Magellan Straits, where Punta Arenas' importance as a colony increased every year, the Chilean republic should have been encouraged to pursue this system, to provoke an exodus of emigrants toward the Magellanic Archipelago's islands now under its dominion, and use this fertile region previously left in the hands of wretched Indian tribes.

Indeed, here at Hoste Island, located in the middle of the southern canal's labyrinth, a large vessel came to put in at the coast under circumstances that the government quickly learned of. The vessel carried nearly one thousand emigrants to an African land grant that had been accorded to Portugal. Yes! On Hoste Island, *The Jonathan*'s wreck had forced a hundred families to seek shelter: men, women, and children from America, Germany, and Ireland. They were part of the overflow of crowded American cities, who urgently prospect for riches in the remotest regions overseas.

The Chilean government told itself that this was an unexpected occasion to transform *The Jonathan*'s castaways into colonists on Hoste Island. They did not send a repatriation vessel, but a sloop stationed at Punta Arenas, in order to make this proposal known. Hoste Island would be placed entirely at their disposal, not by temporary grant but in full ownership, relinquished for the new colonists' benefit.

The proposal was extremely clear, plain, and shrewd. Due to Chile's sacrifice of Hoste Island, in order to ensure its immediate exploitation, perhaps Clarence, Dawson, Navarin, and Hermitte Islands would also receive other emigrants, while remaining under Chilean rule. If the new colony prospered—which seemed likely—it would become known that Magellania's climate was not to be feared, and its agricultural and mineral resources would be known, as well as the fact that the archipelago's pastures and fishing grounds were favorable for setting up colonies, and that its coastal trade was extending farther and farther.

It must be noted that Punta Arenas already had a splendid future as a free port, with no demands or harassment from customs tariffs and open without charge to ships from two continents. This would insure the Chilean republic's dominance over the Magellan Straits, which, although technically neutral, still belonged to Chile on both banks. In a highly political move, the government at Santiago did not stop at making Hoste Island a tax-free zone, but handed over property rights, thereby giving it entire autonomy and separating it from its domain, which made it the only part of Magellania that would enjoy complete independence.

It was a choice that the Argentinean government would not have made, unless they abandoned Tierra del Fuego. The treaty of 1881 had given them no islands, apart from Terre des Etats, which was unproductive and uncultivated, and the Chilean colors waved above the entire archipelago south of Beagle Canal, and west of the Magellan Straits.

It remained to be seen whether *The Jonathan*'s castaways would accept the offer, and exchange the African land grant for Hoste Island, which they would own entirely.

The sloop brought the request and would bring back the response, but the government wanted no delay. They did not intend to leave the question open, and the captain had full powers to deal with representatives chosen by the emigrants. He would remain at anchor for two weeks at Hoste Island, and then leave whether a treaty was signed or not.

If the answer was yes, the new colonists would immediately take possession of Hoste Island, and they could raise whatever flag they pleased there.

If the answer was no, the government would decide about how to repatriate the castaways. Obviously, the two-hundred-ton sloop couldn't carry them, not even as far as Punta Arenas. It would take some time for an American vessel sent from San Francisco by the American company, and several weeks would go by before the island was evacuated.

As might be imagined, the unexpected offer from Santiago created a dramatic effect.

For the first two days, it was the subject of heated discussions among families, without any attempt to talk it over in a public assembly. Many emigrants, finding it too odd, refused to take it seriously. Some of the more competent ones went repeatedly to the captain to ask for explanations, verify his authority, and assure themselves that Hoste Island's independence would be guaranteed by the Chilean republic.

The captain tried everything to convince the parties concerned. He made them understand his government's motives, and how long it would take before a new colony was founded in the Magellanic Archipelago, following the example of Punta Arenas. *The Jonathan*'s castaways were emigrants. They found themselves on Hoste Island. . . . They were offered proprietary rights . . .

"The gift contract is ready," added the captain, "and only needs to be signed."

"By whom?" asked Mr. Rhodes.

"Delegates chosen by the emigrants in a general assembly."

Indeed, this was the only way to proceed. Later on, when the colony organized itself, it would decide whether to name a leader or not. It would freely choose whichever form of government seemed best, and Chile would not interfere with this choice.

Let's examine the situation to better understand the offer.

Who were the passengers picked up by *The Jonathan* in San Francisco for transport to Lagoa Bay? Mostly Americans, Germans, Canadians, and Irish, poor folk who were forced to become expatriates to earn a living. The colonization company obtained a land grant amid Portugal's African territories, but only for a limited time, and the government would not cede its rights to the future colonists. If the latter only thought of their own interests, it mattered little whether they settled in one place or another, so long as their future was assured and life conditions equally favorable.

Since *The Jonathan*'s passengers had reached Hoste Island, an entire winter had gone by; they were able to see for themselves that the climate was moderate, and that the good weather was abundant in a way not always seen at latitudes closer to the equator. In Dominion, British Columbia, on the northern limits of America, the cold lasted longer and was more intense, and the plant life grew later and was less diverse.

By natural instinct, the emigrants wanted to rely on those who distinguished themselves by social rank, education, and intelligence. Mr. Rhodes and a dozen of his companions inspired confidence in heads of families, who consulted them, and freely accepted their influence. At frequent meetings, questions were examined from different angles. The pros and cons were carefully explored.

How unfortunate that Kaw-djer had left Hoste Island precisely when his advice would have been so very welcome! No one could have pointed out the right choice better than he; and he probably would have advised them to accept the Chilean government's proposition, especially because it guaranteed the complete independence of one of the Magellanic Archipelago's eleven major islands. Mr. Rhodes was sure that Kaw-djer would have expressed himself this way, with the authority he had acquired through so many services rendered during the wintering.

In short, after long negotiations and examining arguments from all sides, it became clear that the majority of emigrants were for the Chilean government's offer. Mr. Rhodes was entirely won over by this solution. He and his supporters offered valid explanations. The new colony would belong to them, whereas the one at Lagoa Bay would be under Portuguese rule, not to mention the neighboring British at the Cape, the people at Orange and Pretoria, and the dangers they might run at the outer limits of Kaffraria. Surely, the emigrants had to weigh these risks before negotiating with the colonization company, and they accepted them; but now the opportunity presented itself to establish a colony in better conditions on Hoste Island where they had already lived for eight months. There was no need to take to the sea again, and how long would it take for a vessel to come and transport the emigrants to Lagoa Bay? First, wouldn't they need to dock in some port in Chile or Argentina, in order to avoid a second winter if the vessel did not arrive quickly?

Finally, there was the fact that the government was concerned with the colony's fate. They could count on their help. Regular interaction would begin between Hoste Island and Punta Arenas. New trading posts would open on the shore of the Magellan Straits, and other points along the archipelago. Trade with the Falklands would expand, when the fishing grounds were well organized in these waters. Soon the Argentinean republic would no longer leave the Fuegian territories bordered by Beagle Canal in a state of abandonment. Villages would be set up as rivals to Punta Arenas, and Tierra del Fuego would have its capital, like the Brunswick Peninsula. [That's what happened, and an Argentinean village, Ushaia, now exists on the Beagle Canal: Author's note]

All these arguments were weighty, and they proved decisive. The influence of Mr. Rhodes and a few others won the day.

It must be added that the Merritt brothers and their supporters united from the beginning of the debate. It suited them to stay on the soon-to-be-independent island, in the hopes of better advancing their doctrines. A communally owned property . . . collectivism imposed on emigrants that might lead to anarchism . . . A sheltering land for all the libertarians and supporters of disorder rejected by civilized nations! What a future!

Finally, a vote was called for, as the deadline fixed by the Chilean government was approaching. The sloop's captain urged them to resolve the matter. On the given date, October 29, he would set sail and Chile would retain its rights over Hoste Island.

A general assembly was convened on October 26. A total of 327 adult male emigrants would take part in the final vote, with women and children excluded.

The vote count was 295 in favor of accepting, by far the majority. Only 32 voters were opposed, preferring to stick to the original plan of going to Lagoa Bay. They finally submitted to the majority's will.

That very day the treaty was signed by the captain representing the Chilean government, Mr. Rhodes and nine other delegates representing the future inhabitants of Hoste Island, which was now independent territory.

The next day, a sloop left the Hardy Peninsula docking area, carrying Lieutenant Furner and *The Jonathan*'s crew, who would be repatriated to Punta Arenas by the governor. Only the boatswain Tom Land expressed the desire to stay on the island as a colonist. He was an energetic and trustworthy man, whose skills were admired by Mr. Rhodes, and his request was approved.

Then the Hosteian group began to organize the colony. Unfortunately, although they shared the same name, they still came from different backgrounds and it was difficult to make a melting pot of their rebellious spirits. In powerful nations like the United States of America, or the kingdom of Canada, it is difficult to mix races together, and in the same city Americans remain American,

Germans remain German, and the British remain British— it is impossible to say when if ever a fusion will occur.

Organizing the colony would require a frightful amount of patience, effort, and above all courage and decisiveness.

But the question arose: Who should possess a supreme authority that could not be checked or impeded? Would a committee or a single man be better?

Mr. Rhodes seemed to possess the required qualities for a top-ranking position, by his education—better than most of the other emigrants—and most agreed that his intelligence, good sense, and personal virtues fitted him for exercising power. But he felt that he would be forced to struggle against an intransigent minority, noisy, violent, and ready to revolt, and that despite his energy, he would be overpowered by them.

So a committee would be formed of the worthiest emigrants, presided by Mr. Rhodes if it was so wished, whose members would devote themselves to the common good by accepting responsibilities in a difficult situation.

When he discussed this matter with some of them, he said:

"In the land grant on Lagoa Bay, the situation wasn't what it is here, and organizing would not have met the same obstacles. There the colony would belong directly to Portugal and authority would belong to the Portuguese government."

"Maybe it's unfortunate after all," he was told, "that Chile hasn't imposed a governor on Hoste Island as it did with Punta Arenas . . ."

"In that case, " Mr. Rhodes declared, "it would have remained Chilean and lost its autonomy. We decided to accept the offer in order to belong to no one and to be free in our own home, and in exchange for colonizing Hoste Island, we will assure its independence and our own!"

Truly, Mr. Rhodes' answer had hit the bullseye. It was vital to organize without delay, and at the next meeting, the assembly voted to form a four-member committee, which would include an

American, a German, a Canadian, and an Irishman, presided over by Mr. Rhodes. Americans were the most numerous of the emigrants, so it was natural that their country should be predominant.

First, land ownership had to be dealt with. Hoste Island might have served the needs of twice, or even three times, the number of colonists, as it measured over two hundred square leagues of land mostly suitable for cultivation—forests and pastures. Each family could be given what it required. Farming goods were plentiful, including seeds and plants that *The Jonathan* had carried in great quantities, as well as the necessary agricultural equipment. Most of the emigrants were accustomed to this sort of field labor. As they had done it in their native lands, they expected to do the same in their new country. At first, there were too few domestic animals, but little by little, animals were collected in response to inquiries from the Patagonian territories—where they numbered in the thousands, especially goats—the Argentine pampas, the vast plains of Tierra del Fuego, and the Falkland Islands where sheep were raised abundantly.

Hoste Island's resources were considerable, once past the Hardy Peninsula's beaches along the banks of the Yacana River. It was vital to extend the farmland to the island's center, where the most fertile soil was, to the west up to Rous Point, and to the northeast by way of splendid prairies neighboring the deep notches of Nassau Bay. The colonists would agree to settle in these various areas, and take possession of them; but would they seek to group together by nationality, Americans with Americans, Canadians with Canadians, Germans with Germans, and Irish with Irish; would the committee be powerful enough to insist on the fusion of races, so important for the Hoste colony's future?

Mr. Rhodes and his colleagues had to take care of *The Jonathan's* cargo and energetically intervene to make sure that it was not looted. It must be shared in an equitable way, proportionately according to each family's needs. Above all, there must be no wasting of provisions. This would ensure the colonists' nourishment for a few more months and allow them to get through until they could survive on the island's resources alone.

The committee did everything in its power to act justly and safeguard everyone's rights. Unfortunately, it was soon overwhelmed by demands from different parties about the distribution of grains, preserved meats, and alcoholic beverages, and attempts were made to loot the storehouses containing them. Finally, a resolution was proposed and accepted—over the protests of the Merritt brothers and their gang (as they really must be described), who were to commit violence against people and property; it was decided that the provisions would be kept tin storehouses on the Hardy Peninsula and distributed in small quantities only in case of need to colonists who stayed at the Yacana River campground, which became the colony's main center, as well as those who would be encouraged to settle in the island's other areas.

To divide up the land, it was clear that each colonist intended to choose what he pleased, some wanting to cultivate the earth, others to exploit the forests that were rich in wood for construction and much-needed fuel, unless Hoste Island contained coal mines, as did the Brunswick Peninsula near Punta Arenas. And some of the colonists sought pasture ground for raising livestock.

The most coveted lands were those along the banks of the Yacana River, near the village-in-progress. The committee was challenged by the Merritt brothers' latest violent manner of advocating the deadly laws of collectivism. They refused to divide up the ground and insisted that the land be used for communal profit. Such was the unyielding collectivism that they hoped to impose, and if any colonist made a profit outside the community, anyone would have the right to rob him of it for the benefit of everyone.

The committee needed to act energetically, faced by such doctrines held by violent men. It resolved to put down by force any attempts at revolt. The struggle was primarily against about twenty

German and Irish families, a total of one hundred and fifty people who were the most ardent protesters for anarchism and supporters of the Merritt brothers.

The question was a vital one, on which Hoste Island's future depended. Either the party of order, in the majority, would win, or the party of disorder, ready to go to any lengths. The Merritt brothers did not expect to take their rightful part of the cargo and equipment, then move to some other part of the island to live as they wished. No! They wanted to live in the growing village, turning it into a hive for drones, forcing others to put up with their rule, in short to act as masters, although they claimed not to recognize any masters.

Mr. Rhodes and his friends were resolved to resist them, fighting violence with violence. Rather than accept this abominable social condition, they would appeal to the Chilean government, requesting that Hoste Island's independence be restored, and they would abandon it, never to return.

Only one man might have been able to govern at this dangerous time when words became deeds. This man was especially appreciated, because he had been observed at work. The Merritt brothers were aware that he was close to them in theory, and they sensed in him a spirit rebellious to all authority.

That man was Kaw-djer. But what had happened to him? There was no news of him since he left in the longboat. Were they even sure he had gone to New Island to take up his former life with Karroly? Would he have accepted the request to intervene, and in what manner? Wouldn't he remain faithful to the radical ideas for which he had sacrificed his entire life?

But he wasn't there—and was there any hope of his reappearing?

The crisis reached an acute phase, and from hour to hour, the two sides were expected to come to violence.

Mr. Rhodes and his committee colleagues hoped for one last possibility, that a vessel would arrive in view of the island. Two months had gone by since the sloop left, and following the request of the Punta Arenas governor, Chile should have taken steps to send a ship to Hoste Island to bring the domestic animals that were needed.

It was December thirteenth, the middle of summer. Surely the expected ship would anchor at the Yacana River's mouth, before the good weather was over.

That day, it wasn't the ship that was spotted in the west. It was a longboat, which, coming from the east, went around the tip of False Cape Horn.

It was immediately identified as the *Wel-Kiej,* piloted by Karroly and his son, Halg, one at the rudder and the other at the sails . . .

But was Kaw-djer aboard? . . .

XIII

A LEADER

Nearly two months before this day, on the evening when he saw the Chilean sloop approaching, Kaw-djer left Hoste Island without telling anyone, not even Mr. Rhodes or his family, to whom he was sincerely attached. Where did he go, and did he even know where he was going?

During the night, turning round the farthest rocks of Hardy Peninsula, Karroly and his son maneuvered to go northward with a small breeze from the west, heading to New Island.

Would Kaw-djer return to the home he had abandoned since mid-February and return to his charitable trips among the Fuegian tribes?

No! Could Kaw-djer forget the treaty that was signed between Chile and Argentina? No matter how far he fled, to the farthest reaches of Magellania, could he ever find an island, islet, or rock that didn't belong to one or another of the two republics? No matter what part of the archipelago he set foot on henceforth, could he ever escape laws that he wanted no part of? Since there was reason to believe that the Punta Arenas governor was concerned about him and was determined to find out the secrets of his past, would he be sought, pursued, and tracked down by agents? Would he return to the farthest point of Cape Horn . . . and then what? How had things changed? During the few weeks he had just spent on Hoste Island his heart, formerly closed to almost all human affection, had opened once again. And after having saved *The Jonathan*'s castaways, he had once again felt tied to the world and humanity, to the Rhodes family, and a few others.

A month after his departure the longboat reached the New Island cove. Kaw-djer had intended to return there without putting in anywhere else. But in following Beagle Canal's northern bank, he could not refuse to visit some Tierra del Fuego campgrounds. How could he resist appeals by the Indians, whose canoes came alongside the *Wel-kiej*? The unfortunate Pecherais were overjoyed to see their benefactor again. And in some tribes women and children needed his care . . .

The Argentine flag flew over different parts of the coast, which pained and enraged him. The Buenos Aires government had already taken possession. The Chilean colors doubtless flew over the various islands of southern Magellania that belonged to Chile.

Who knows what went on in Kaw-djer's heart when he returned to New Island, at the tip's edge, and saw the red and white flag unfurling in the wind!

So the Chilean agents had come! His home had been visited by them, for he found the door open. Had he been there, they would have grabbed him and interrogated him . . . and when he refused to reply, they would have taken him to Punta Arenas . . .

No! It was impossible! He would abandon New Island, and he thought again of seeking in death, which is nevertheless not an eternal sleep, the rest that life could not give him!

But this time, he would not take the route of Cape Horn. What use in going so far? The sea beat against the rocks of New Island just as at the Cape. One day he would disappear, after having thrown the detested flag into the waves, and Karroly would look for him in vain throughout the island . . .

Such were Kaw-djer's resolutions, which neither the Indian nor his son could have guessed. However, two weeks went by without his acting on his plan. Perhaps the pull of memories still held him back?

* * *

During the day of December third, news came of a kind to make him change his plans.

On that day, one of the Indians from the Wallah campground came in his canoe to ask for help, telling him about what had happened at Hoste Island, about the Chilean government's proposals that had been accepted by the emigrants, the land grant that had been made to them, the island becoming independent again, alone in the entire archipelago.

Was the Indian in error, and how had he learned this news?

"No, Kaw-djer," he said. "Father Athanase told us about it at the campground . . ."

"When? . . ."

"Three days ago."

"And he got it from? . . ."

"Agents from Argentina who visited the mission!"

The Indian's answers were so decisive that there was no reason to doubt the accuracy of the news.

It affected Kaw-djer like a call back to life. His constricted chest expanded, as if he allowed himself to breathe again.

He proposed to Karroly that they abandon their home on New Island and everything they owned to go to Hoste Island, to become the pilot for the new colony, whose brilliant future Kaw-djer glimpsed; and the proposal was instantly accepted. At this time of the season, the last furs had been sold to traffickers. The longboat would suffice for carrying the necessary equipment. This task took three days, and after a visit to the Wallah campground, the *Wel-kiej* followed Beagle Canal, the Navarin Channel, and on December thirteenth, put in at Hoste Island.

When Kaw-djer debarked, he was greeted with cheers from the colonists who ran along the shore.

Kaw-djer had to know that he was popular in the Hoste colony, but he could not understand why his popularity seemed to have increased.

Right after his debarkation, he found the Rhodes family and his first words were:

"Hoste is independent?"

"Hurrah, hurrah, hurrah!" shouted the crowd of colonists.

After exchanging handshakes and squeezing Mr. Rhodes in his arms and kissing the young boy and young girl, Kaw-djer followed them to their home.

Everyone could see that this welcome gave him great joy, for he was smiling, instead of his habitually sad expression.

"Finally," he said, "I'll be able to stay among you, my friends, and from now on my life will be yours!"

This seemed like the happiness of a man wearied by a long and painful road, who had just achieved his goal and could finally rest.

"Yes, my friend," Mr. Rhodes told him, "here you are back at Hoste Island, when we feared we might never see you again, and we hope it isn't too late!"

These words were said in such a tone of discouragement that Kaw-djer's heart was overwhelmed, and he felt confronted by a highly menacing predicament.

Just then, two of Mr. Rhodes' colleagues entered, Messrs. O'Nark and Broks. Kaw-djer looked from one to the other, and then Mr. Rhodes told him in a trembling voice:

"My friend, the God you don't believe in has brought you back here to save us all! Our unfortunate colony threatened by the worst disorder, and perhaps the Chilean government's only choice will be to repossess the island . . ."

"Repossess it?" shouted Kaw-djer in a frightening voice.

He stood up, with lightening flashing in his eyes, his feet stamping the ground as if he wished to be rooted there.

"My friend," Mr. Rhodes continued, "since you left some serious things have happened. Chile has completely ceded Hoste Island to us, if we colonize it. The proposal was accepted by a near-unanimous vote. *The Jonathan*'s castaways found it advantageous from every point of view, and gave up the plan to set up a colony on African soil."

"What better thing could have happened?" interrupted Kaw-djer, incapable of holding back the thoughts boiling inside him. At

Lagoa Bay, they would have had to submit to foreign rule. They would have been dependent on the Portuguese authorities. Here, on newly free territory, there were no masters.

"Kaw-djer," said one of Mr. Rhodes' colleagues in a determined voice, "is the exactly the leader we need . . . He would have the right, and the mandate, to make himself obeyed . . ."

"A leader!" said Kaw-djer, who was revolted by the word.

"A chief, if you prefer, my friend," replied Mr. Rhodes, "a chief invested with sufficient authority to administrate our colony, to distribute to each person what is rightfully his, to impose the law on those who do not wish to obey them; in short, to govern in the name of everyone and in everyone's interest."

Kaw-djer listened silently, his head bowed.

"And instead, what have we had?" continued Mr. Rhodes. "Confusion, upheavals, disarray, the risk of falling into the worst anarchy, attempts at looting that threaten to destroy our resources, which could compromise our colony's future and lead to its ruin!"

"You understand, Kaw-djer," added Mrs. Rhodes.

Outside there was an uproar, but not the hurrahs shouted when the longboat returned.

Did Kaw-djer hear the noise outside? Did it signify the defeat of all his ideas? Was what he dreamed upon returning to Hoste Island impossible, to socialize the new colony's productive powers, with wealth shared by the collectivity, and lives devoted to work without hindrances or chains, where no higher authority whatsoever intervened—in short, would he have to renounce the theories he hoped to try out fairly, would the situation be saved only by the power of authoritarianism?

He learned from Mr. Rhodes that the organizational committee was overwhelmed in its fight against the anarchistic doctrines the minority was trying to impose upon the majority. He realized that things were going from bad to worse daily and that a catastrophe was imminent. The Merritt brothers' actions, as well as those of the Irish and Germans allied with them, were recounted. They wanted the island to submit to a regime that, while claiming solidarity, was the most tyrannical of all . . . They refused to obey the committee's orders. They incited their supporters to loot the storehouses, seize goods, and spread out over the island those colonists who were resolved not to obey them, perhaps to scare them off. Mr. Rhodes kept exclaiming a single word, like a curse:

"Anarchy! . . . Anarchy!"

Now that he was confronting a threatening situation, was this word still dear to Kaw-djer? Were his former beliefs shaken? In his mind, so intransigent about the realities of social government, so set against all the evidence of the way things work, was a gap created through which wiser and more practical ideas could penetrate?

He remained motionless—perhaps because a supreme struggle was going on inside him—and turned his head away. Feeling that all eyes were on him, he retained a rebellious attitude and kept fiercely silent.

Mr. Rhodes took his hand, and Mrs. Rhodes and the two children surrounded him more closely. Messrs. O'Nark and Broks approached and their colleague continued:

"No, my friend, no, nothing can be accomplished, nothing can even work in a society where each man is master of his own will, his fancy, or his whim. Nothing stable or definitive can be founded when a higher leader is lacking. A superior head for thinking and a hand for action is required. Without this head and this hand, we are lost, and we might as well abandon our island to the mercy of the violent men who, after having run us off, will finally devour themselves, which is the inevitable result of revolutionary excess!"

Mr. Rhodes and his family knew of Kaw-djer's doctrines about these serious subjects, how he reproached modern society, and the new social state he dreamed of beyond any human or divine dominion. They also knew that he was not a sectarian who sought to impose his will by violence, armed with iron and fire. Was it possible that he would act in contradiction with his own beliefs?

"My friend," Mr. Rhodes continued insistently, "when we are forced to work for everyone, work becomes an unbearable task, as we quickly become the dupe of evil and lazy people! Communism would be workable if men had the same ideas about everything, the same tastes, hopes, intelligence and turn of mind, the same physical and moral strength. But things are not that way, and humanity is made up of diverse and irreconcilable elements. That's why communism must end in the void of anarchy!"

As if a burden weighed on his shoulders, Kaw-djer sat in a corner of the room with his head in his hands. What was he thinking? Would he answer Mr. Rhodes' remarks, and how? Would he recognize the upheavals Hoste Island was undergoing? Did he foresee its ruin in the near future, its abandonment to the Merritt brothers and their gang, then Chile's intervention to get rid of these wretches, and finally, its loss of independence to Chilean rule?

What would become of Kaw-djer, who thought he had found a secure refuge on the island, the only independent one in the Magellanic Archipelago? Here was new quicksand under his feet, and when the colonists fled to the Lagoa Bay land grant, where would he go?

Just then the shouts grew louder, shouts of fury from one side and terror from another. The rioters approached, threatening the village. Mr. Rhodes and the committee members had to face the rebels. Their supporters surrounded the house and called for them.

"Come," said Mr. Rhodes to his colleagues. "Our place is with them!"

He went to the door and stopped at the threshold, turning toward Kaw-djer.

Terrified by the growing clamor, at the moment when Mr. Rhodes was going to open the door and his son, O'Nark, and Broks were ready to follow him, Mrs. Rhodes and her daughter threw themselves at Kaw-djer's knees; taking his hand with beseeching looks, they cried in tremulous voices, "You . . . you . . . our savior!"

Could he save them the entire population, which was threatened by the anarchist gang? The committee was powerless; would he succeed when his only support was his popularity? They needed a leader, a leader whose bravery equaled his energy. Did he have the makings of a leader, and should he devote himself to the common good, or give up this duty that circumstances imposed upon him, when he had fulfilled it?

"Kaw-djer!" Mr. Rhodes shouted one last time, "in the name of all these brave people whom neither my colleagues nor myself can help, I call upon you to be our leader!"

At this moment, a crowd of women and children came toward Mr. Rhodes' house.

Farther off, echoed shouts drew nearer:

"To the storehouses . . . To the storehouses!"

It was time to face facts. The Merritt brothers, after invading the village with nearly two hundred rebels, headed for the colony's storehouses. Shouts of "To the storehouses!" came from those who wanted to attack them, not those who wanted to defend them.

The latter were joined by Messrs. Rhodes, O'Nark, and Broks, now armed with rifles, to prevent looting.

Through the open door, many frightened colonists could be seen, going to the foot of the bluff, and some even went to the little cove, where the longboat was anchored, with Karroly and his son aboard.

One last time, after having crossed the threshold of his house, Mr. Rhodes paused and his voice rang out:

"Kaw-djer!" he shouted.

Suddenly, Kaw-djer rose, his head held high, his cheeks ruddy and eyes aflame. He took some steps to the door, but stopped just before going out.

He observed the riot's full-scale tumult on the square, a group of women and children fleeing toward the bluff, around a hundred men lined up around the storehouses, which had to be protected at all cost against looters; less than two hundred feet away along the left bank of the Yacana River was a roaring mob led by John and Jack Merritt, most of them armed with rifles and revolvers.

"Hurrah . . . Hurrah for Jack Merritt!" they bellowed.

After their last appeal to Kaw-djer, Messrs. Rhodes, O'Nark, and Broks hurried toward the storehouses, where their committee colleagues awaited them.

At this moment, the rebels, instead of going in that direction, maneuvered to surround them. They wanted to take hold of them, force them to give up the jobs they had been elected to do, and then replace them with one of the Merritt brothers as the island's sole leader, making the entire colony recognize his authority. That's what the cheers for Jack Merritt meant!

When the Merritt brothers were only a few steps away, ahead of the mob, they paused.

"What do you want?" asked Mr. Rhodes.

"You and your colleagues must resign," replied John Merritt.

"No! . . . We won't!"

Roars greeted this statement, as the two groups closed in, ready to fight. Each side aimed rifles and steadied revolvers, ready to fire.

From the tumultuous rebel mob, the shouts came louder: "Hurrah! Hurrah for Jack Merritt!"

He was the more violent of the two brothers, with an athlete's build and exceptional energy, capable of every excess and worthy of leading a colony of evildoers.

At a gesture from him, a dozen of his supporters marched toward Mr. Rhodes and his colleagues. If they refused to resign, they would be forced to do so, by whatever form of violence necessary.

Mr. Rhodes, with his colleagues nearby, was surrounded by friends, determined to defend him. The fight was about to begin. The first gunshot would be followed by fifty others.

Suddenly, a powerful voice resounded amid the tumult:

"Put your guns down!"

Kaw-djer had just appeared on the house's threshold. He came forward, and the crowd made way for him. His height and entire aspect inspired sympathy and demanded respect.

The only man capable of dominating the situation had appeared, capable of forcing the rebels to return to order, capable of damming up their hateful demands, capable of stopping the fight just when blood was about to flow.

At the sight of him, there was a pause. Even the most determined men hesitated. The Merritt brothers stepped back a few feet.

"Kaw-djer! . . . Kaw-djer!" Hundreds of voices cheered.

Karroly and his son came forward, both armed with rifles and ready to kill in order to defend Kaw-djer if his life were threatened.

Mr. Rhodes and his colleagues made room, and Kaw-djer took his place among them.

In a calm and strong voice that betrayed no emotion:

"What do you want?" he asked the rebels.

"What we want," answered John Merritt, "is for the committee to resign! And a leader chosen by us!"

"Who would he be?"

"Someone who shares our ideas, and who can organize the colony the way we want! My brother!"

"Yes . . . Hurrah for Jack Merritt!"

The howls grew louder, stopping only when Kaw-djer, stepping to the front row, replied:

"The leader is the committee, and everyone must obey it!"

"No!" shouted Jack Merritt, a man of action more than of words, heading toward Mr. Rhodes.

"One more step . . . ," said Kaw-djer.

Grabbing the rifle from Karroly, who was next to him, he aimed it.

The other guns lowered. Had Kaw-djer's intervention only delayed the bloodshed?

Then Mr. Rhodes called for silence with a gesture:

"This resignation you're calling for," he declared, "the committee refuses, since you have no right to demand it of me. Speaking for the committee, I do it freely and voluntarily for a man who is the most worthy to be our leader, the man whom all Magellania salutes with the name of benefactor!"

Through an irrepressible accord, made of trust and gratitude, a shout went up from every side, even from among the rebels:

"Hurrah for Kaw-djer . . . hurrah!"

Kaw-djer raised his hand and said:

"Do you want me as your leader?"

"We want him!" Mr. Rhodes and his colleagues declared, stretching out their arms to him.

"Hurrah!" repeated the vast majority of colonists.

"So be it!" replied Kaw-djer.

Those were the circumstances in which he became leader of Hoste Island, which he protected, and whose independence he defended.

XIV

SIX YEARS OF PROSPERITY

Six years after the events just described, sailing in Hoste Island's waters no longer presented any of the previous difficulties or dangers. A ship could sail from point to point in perfect safety, whether to Beagle Canal, Darwin Sound, or even the edge of Hardy Peninsula across Cape Horn Archipelago. At the peninsula's tip, a warning fire shone out in several directions on the open sea—not one of the Pecherais' fires like those in the campgrounds of Fuegian territory, but a port fire, lighting the channels and allowing passing ships to avoid being thrown against the reefs on dark winter nights.

At the entrance to the creek fed by the Yacana River, some piers served as breakwaters, and the wharfs allowed ships, sheltered from squalls, to unload their cargoes and load up for long-distance trips. The port was developed little by little, through business contacts established between Hoste Island, Chile, and Argentina. They extended as far as the old and new continents.

Beyond the port, on the two banks of the waterway joined by a wooden bridge, a village developed, which would soon become a city. Symmetrical streets had been outlined, at right angles to one another in the American style, lined with houses made of stone and wood, with yard in front and small gardens in back. Some squares were shaded by fine trees, mostly beeches, and others with indeciduous leaves. Here and there several larger buildings stood, the governor's home, used for diverse public functions, and a church whose belltower appeared among the foliage at the foot of the bluff.

In 1882 to 1883, when the French mission, transported by the ship *La Romanche*, anchored at Hoste Island's Orange Bay to observe the planet Venus passing by, its contacts with the new colony left it with excellent memories.

A seaman forced to put in around these waters without exactly measuring his position would surely have wondered if he had reached Punta Arenas, if this was the Brunswick Peninsula, and if the west winds had pushed him through the Magellan Straits.

No! It was Hoste Island. The village in question was Liberia, the capital of the island that had been given six years earlier to *The Jonathan*'s castaways.

Such was the result obtained in a few years, thanks to the energy, intelligence, and practical mind of the leader named by the Hosteians when anarchy was leading the island to ruin. Not only had it been saved from this fate, but it had also avoided Chilean rule.

However, Kaw-djer was as unknown as ever, and no one dreamed of asking him about his past. All that anyone knew, and that seemed enough, was that long ago, he came to find refuge in the Magellanic Archipelago, he lived on New Island with the pilot Karroly, and devoted his life to the Magellania's poor natives. Mr. Rhodes felt it was probable that Kaw-djer had such an unyielding personality, so stubborn about social questions, that he could never have submitted to any authority whatsoever. As we know, he was not mistaken.

The Jonathan's passengers could not forget either that they owed their salvation to Kaw-djer. At the worst of the storm, he had lit a fire on the summit of Cape Horn, risked his life to sail alongside the disabled ship, which the squall was pushing toward the reefs, and brought a pilot who was the only one capable of negotiating the perilous channels and leading them to the shelter of Hoste Island in the middle of that dark night.

No one had forgotten the services rendered, and for this very reason, on the day when Mr. Rhodes and his colleagues ceded their responsibilities, a large majority voted in favor of Kaw-djer. All defenders of order united for him, greeting him with cheers, and even some of the Merritt brothers' supporters split from their gang.

Such was the man's influence. A sort of magical power wafted from his body, and when the committee resigned, naming him as universally elected leader, Mr. Rhodes knew with his good sense that only this man could maintain order and manage the organizational work.

Is it possible that Kaw-djer had an unlikely change of mind, throwing out his previous ideas, and had returned to a more normal notion of nature's requirements of mankind?

In any case, we know he arrived at that point by a series of disappointments. Some months earlier, he thought that there was no place left for him, that he couldn't find shelter anywhere on earth. He was thrown out of Magellania, where he had hoped to stay until the end of his life, when the archipelago became part of a government that would bend him under its yoke and punish him with a goad.

As soon as he discovered that Hoste Island kept its independence, Kaw-djer quickly left his islet, which had become Chilean, to rejoin the little world of colonists and live among them.

He thought that the organizational work had to be very advanced, if not completed, by this time, but he would arrive in time to participate, adding his personal imprint to make sure that total freedom, which he believed every human deserved, would exist, without a shadow of authority ever making itself felt.

But when the longboat debarked on the shore of Hardy Peninsula, he discovered total disarray: honest men threatened by evildoers, a roaring riot with revolutionaries impatient to go looting, and blood about to stain the ground of Hoste Island.

Then a leader needed to be named—a single leader, who could maintain order . . . and he accepted to be this leader.

The same day, in Mr. Rhodes' house, the latter thanked him, saying:

"My friend, you saved us from the greatest misfortunes, of which the worst would be to have to leave our island! . . . You saved our independence, and you are a godsend!"

That he had been sent on a providential mission was of course unacceptable for this dissenter against all divine power. But he did not challenge the statement, only saying:

"I accepted the task of organizing the colony . . . I will apply myself to doing so, and once finished, my mandate will be over. I hope I will have proved that there is at least one place on earth where man needs no master! . . ."

"A leader isn't a master, my friend," declared Mr. Rhodes, "and you are going to prove it. But every society needs a higher authority, whatever name it is called by, which must have the necessary power to govern."

"In any case," Kaw-djer responded, "this authority must end as soon as the community has been organized, giving everyone his independence."

"So be it, my friend, but you have full powers, and I know you'll use them for the common good. To work, then, and from the start, protect our colony's future, even if it takes force! . . . And your own future too, because you are a citizen of Hoste Island!"

Kaw-djer began to work ardently, and even though the committee had been dissolved and power placed in the hands of one man, its members offered their help, which he was quick to accept.

Most vital was to reestablish order in the colony, to guarantee the security of property and individuals, and to safeguard the stored goods that were common property. But peace could not reign over the island as long as the rebel party remained and a certain number of anarchists followed the Merritt brothers, so long as the libertarians were not rendered powerless. Highly energetic action was needed against these enemies of society.

From the day Kaw-djer became the Hosteian colony's leader, John and Jack Merritt saw him as the man chosen to fight them, the enemy of their antisocial doctrines, who must be brought down at all costs and by any means. They may have suspected that until then, Kaw-djer had shared their ideas, at least theoretically, and they may have hoped he would put them to practical use. But their error was short-lived, and they quickly realized that they couldn't count on him.

Since the new leader was named, the Merritt brothers had only around fifty supporters left, resolved to follow them to the end—most were Germans of the Karl Marx school, or Irishmen pushed to extreme violence by the Sinn Fein movement. They were a minority, which should have inspired a certain prudence in them. For their own good, it was better that they set up on another part of Hoste Island, where perhaps Kaw-djer would allow them to try out their utopia, which would soon lead to poverty and ruin. But so overexcited were these misled minds that they tried armed combat the very next day, attacking the storehouses, whose looting would have compromised the colony's future.

Kaw-djer, having assembled the forces of order, quickly quashed the rebellion almost without bloodshed. But a few offenders lost their freedom, among others the Merritt brothers, who were imprisoned under surveillance until their fate could be ruled upon.

Faced with this powerful response, most of the rebels surrendered. They were mere members of an anarchist body that no longer had a head.

Kaw-djer quickly decided about Jack and John Merritt. He rejected the idea of forming a kind of tribunal, calling a jury by lots, bringing out the guilty, and waiting for a verdict.

Kaw-djer already knew what the two brothers would tell a jury to defend themselves. They would invoke man's independence and the right not to submit to any authority, a right that masters do not recognize. They would argue that on free soil no law could be applied to those who did not make the law, and that they rejected this dictatorship by one man imposed on the entire Hosteian colony!

These had, after all, been Kaw-djer's own ideas, summing up his doctrines, and now that he had a cure of souls, he sensed their injustice and inanity.

When Mr. Rhodes suggested that they prosecute the guilty men with a jury of colonists, he answered resolutely:

"I don't think we should do so until we have laws to base a judgment on and judges to administer it. These rebels' actions demand quick justice that serves as an example to whoever wants to follow their lead. They must be expelled from the island, never to set foot on it again!"

"You're right, and everyone will agree with you," replied Mr. Rhodes.

"The longboat will take them to Punta Arenas where they will be repatriated at their own convenience."

This was the first official act by Hoste Island's new leader. Pleas by the Merritt brothers and five or six accomplices arrested with them were useless. For the sake of public order, the island had to be rid of these sectarians as quickly as possible.

However, the *Wel-kiej* would not be used for this transport. Three days later, a ship from Valparaiso anchored at the island with extra supplies, a full cargo of items needed by the colonists, and one hundred head of livestock. The government was highly interested in this colonization attempt and cooperated financially; they promised to be of the utmost help. They sent the ship, which after unloading would take to the seas with the rebels expelled from Hoste Island aboard.

After this day, calm reigned in the colony, which was slowly organized by Kaw-djer's strict rule. He was usefully seconded by Mr. Rhodes and a few others, who gladly devoted themselves to the task. They received precious help from *The Jonathan*'s boatswain, Tom Land, who had chosen to stay on the island. He was a resourceful, stubborn man, who saw no difference between a ship and a colony in terms of discipline, where the captain or governor had to be master, second only to God.

First, Kaw-djer wanted to explore the entire island. As we know, its central part offered a large expanse of fertile land, easily cultivated, which would produce an excellent crop in one year's time. Near the Hardy Peninsula and to the north, it was bordered by a densely wooded series of hills that protected it from strong wind and severe cold.

The lands were fairly distributed among the colonists, whose personal property they became. There was no question of putting them under collectivist rule. Each family owned its part, and the profits belonged to them, without the community demanding a share.

"You see, Kaw-djer," Tom Land said while they crossed the shore from False Cape Horn to the tip of Rous Point, "when I save my pay, it's not for my pal who has spent his on food so he can drink mine up! What I earn or save belongs only to me, otherwise I wouldn't work and would just be supported by everyone else. Anyone who thinks otherwise has no idea of what is fair and convenient, and in my view he should be locked in the bilge!"

After Magellania and Patagonia were divided, the two neighboring republics had different approaches to land use. Argentina, uninformed about the region, made land grants of up to ten and twelve leagues in length; with forests that contained up to four thousand trees per hectare [2.47 acres], it took a long time to exploit an area that should have produced 200,000 feet of planking annually. The same was true of farmland and pastures, which were offered to too many lessees, and which needed too many workers and agricultural equipment.

Moreover, the Argentinean colonists were obliged to have constant, difficult, and costly contacts with Buenos Aires. Before merchandise arrived at Magellania, the list of a ship's contents had to be submitted to the Buenos Aires customs office, 1,500 miles away, and six months would go by before it was returned, noting the fees to be paid according to the current market valuations. As economists have written, to speak of Buenos Aires in Tierra del Fuego was like mentioning China or Japan.

On the contrary, Chile was active in encouraging trade and emigrants, beyond the brave attempt at Hoste Island. It founded Punta Arenas, which was declared a free port, so that ships brought quality surplus items and necessities there for purchase at surprising savings. All the products from Argentinean Magellania flowed into Punta Arenas, where British and Chilean companies opened prosperous branches.

For a long time, Kaw-djer knew about the Chilean system of government, and during his lengthy trips across Magellanic territory, he noted that the results of their hunting, fishing, and farming went to Punta Arenas and not Buenos Aires. For this reason Hoste Island was given a free port, following the Chilean colony's example. This free port was the castaways' former campground, which gradually developed from a village to a city under the name of Liberia.

Almost unbelievably, the Argentine republic, which founded Ushaia on Tierra del Fuego, almost exactly above Hoste Island on the other side of Beagle Canal, would not profit from this double example. Compared to Liberia and Punta Arenas, its colony did not develop due to government restrictions on business development, high customs fees, and gold mining restrictions, which smugglers flaunted freely since the governor could not watch over the seven hundred kilometers of coastline under his jurisdiction.

The Hoste Island events, its independent status as granted by Chile, and ever-increasing prosperity under Kaw-djer's firm administration, brought it to the attention of the industrial and business worlds. New colonists were attracted there, who were given land grants under favorable conditions. It was quickly learned that the abundant forests had wood superior to Europe's, yielding up to fifteen or twenty percent more, which led to the building of sawmills and gave birth to a lucrative industry. At the same time, farmers paid one thousand piastres per square league for agricultural use, and soon several thousand livestock were at pasture on the island.

The population rose rapidly. The few hundred castaways from *The Jonathan* were augmented by an almost equal number of emigrants, mostly from the American West, Chile, and Argentina. Two years after independence was declared, Liberia had nearly two thousand inhabitants, and Hoste Island nearly three thousand.

Marriages were soon celebrated in Liberia. The marriage license office was located in city hall, where many other services were also offered, including island security, which was entrusted to reliable officers supervised by Tom Land, the boatswain entirely trusted by Kaw-djer.

Among the notable marriages were those of Marc and Clary Rhodes. Marc wed the daughter of a prosperous sawmill owner, and Clary married a young San Franciscan doctor who settled in Liberia at Kaw-djer's request. Other unions were created from the strong ties between prominent families.

Now, in good weather, the Liberian port received many ships. Coastal trade did excellent business, not only with Liberia, but also with different trading posts established on other points of the island, whether near Rous Point, or the northern shores that are washed by Beagle Canal. They were mostly ships from the Falklands Archipelago, whose routes were extended further each year.

Not only did ships import and export goods from the British islands of the Atlantic, sailboats and steamers came also from Valparaiso, Buenos Aires, Montevideo, and Rio de Janeiro. And in every nearby channel, in Nassau Bay, at Darwin Sound, and on Beagle Canal there floated ships from Denmark, Norway, and America.

The traffic grew dramatically around the many fisheries, which always yielded excellent results in Magellanic waters. This industry was severely regulated by Kaw-djer's guidelines. It was forbidden to exhaust or render extinct—through overkilling—

the supply of any of the numerous sea animals that inhabited these seas. Yacanas, Pecherais, and Fuegians based on Hoste Island passionately pursued this trade; there were also professional sea lion hunters of every origin, adventurers of all kinds, stateless people whom Tom Land was able to hold in check with military-style discipline. Sea lion hunters worked in better conditions than before. There were no more trips at shared expense to some desert island where they often died of fatigue and famine. Now they were assured that they could move the goods they hunted without waiting for months for a ship, which sometimes didn't come. The way of slaughtering the harmless amphibians had not changed, however. Nothing could be simpler: *salir a dar una paliza*—hit them with a stick, as there was no need to use other arms against the poor animals.

In addition to fisheries augmented by the slaughter of sea lions, there were whaling expeditions, always lucrative in these waters. Annually, the archipelago's canals yielded one thousand whales. Ships equipped for this fishing frequented the neighboring channels of Hoste Island in good weather, sure of finding at the Liberia free port all of the advantages offered at Punta Arenas.

Another form of business was to exploit the beaches, which were covered by billions of shells of every kind. Among others, there were myillones, edible mollusks of excellent quality and unimaginable abundance. Ships loaded up on them and sold them for up to five piastres per kilogram in South American cities. The Hoste Island coves harbored the centoya, a giant crab that feeds off underwater algae, crustaceans so large that two furnished a day's food for a hungry fisherman.

These crabs were not the only crustaceans present. There were lobster, crayfish, and mussels, which were canned in factories to be sent overseas.

As expected, the Hoste colony attracted missionaries. They were already present at diverse points of Tierra del Fuego, belonging to Allen Gordon's Mission [Captain Allen Gardiner, who died in 1850 in southern Tierra del Fuego, created the Protestant missions in this land: Editor's note], much venerated locally. The Magellanic territory's Indians were eager for religious lessons, and attended school and church with remarkable devotion.

Allen Gordon's Mission, currently led by Bishop Laurence, managed to attract them by artful methods; sermons were given in their own language, and some Bible passages were translated into Yaghon and handed out widely as booklets.

The Anglican missionaries designed a special hell for the Fuegians, a frozen one. As the poor folk considered the cold as their worst enemy, traditional hellfires would not have scared them as much.

Whatever Kaw-djer's opinions on religion, he politely welcomed the ministers brought by the mission's cutters. He let them move into Liberia and posed no obstacle to religious worship.

He had already reconsidered other notions that were seductive in theory, but did not stand up in practical application. The settlers were glad when, on one of Liberia's public squares a church was built, and schools where Protestant families could send their children.

There were some Catholics from Ireland, Canada, and even America. Missionaries were needed to preach that religion. Churches in Magellania were called upon; their staff hurried over, along with several nuns from the St. Anne monastery, to attend to the sick.

The first to debark at Liberia were Fathers Athanase and Severin, who had last met Kaw-djer at the Wallah campground on Tierra del Fuego. Although he always avoided all contact with missionaries, he knew these were honest and courageous men, as well as conscientious and zealous priests—worthy of the great religion they represented, they fought against the slightly too commercialized proselytism of the Protestant ministers.

In its second year as a colony, Liberia had a Catholic school as comfortable as its rivals, and a church built on the right bank of the Yacana River, with architectural style less severe although not less religious than the strongly puritanical Protestant church.

The representatives of both sects got along amicably, and nothing more troubled the colony that had been threatened at the start by enemies of social order.

What relations existed between Hoste Island and the Chilean government now that all claims on the former had been renounced? They were excellent on both sides. Chile could only congratulate itself more each year for its decision. It gained moral and material profits that the Argentinean republic was still lacking, given its insistence on methods condemned by good economists, whose deplorable effects were already visible in the Ushaia colony.

At first, the Chilean government did not hide its worry and discontent to see as Hoste Island's leader the mysterious character whose presence in the Magellanic Archipelago seemed suspicious. On the independent land where he took refuge, Kaw-djer could no longer be hunted down, nor could his identity or past be determined, since he would not reveal them.

Had he remained on New Island, he would not have escaped the Chilean police, and his attitude proved he was incapable of living under the yoke of any authority; he had rebelled against all society's laws, and perhaps he had been expelled from countries equipped with fair and necessary laws, no matter what the regime. But after the new colony's troubles provoked by anarchistic violence, followed by the expulsion of the Merritt brothers and their gang, calm was reborn on the island thanks to Kaw-djer's firm administration. With business resuming and growing, and with prosperity spreading, there was nothing to do but leave Hoste Island alone. And so, relations were unclouded between the governors of Hoste Island and Punta Arenas.

Given the maritime importance of Liberia's port and its location between Darwin Sound and Nassau Bay, commercial vessels preferred docking there. They found it an excellent port of call, safer than the Chilean colony's, which was visited mainly by steamers crossing the Magellan Straits to go from one ocean to the other.

Karroly, who had become chief pilot for Hoste Island, was

much in demand by ships heading for Punta Arenas, or the trading posts set up on some of the archipelago's islands. He did not wish to abandon his old job, and his son, who had recently married a young Canadian woman, still helped him on board the faithful *Wel-kiej*. They were still devoted body and soul to their benefactor, as if they were all still living in the solitude of New Island.

Six years went by, during which Hoste Island never stopped developing. Kaw-djer's administration had made it a model colony, and three other villages were established to compete with Liberia—a productive and fruitful competition—at Rous Point, at the back of Nassau Bay, and at Darwin Sound's tip, facing Gordon Island. They naturally enhanced the capital, and Kaw-djer traveled there either by sea or by roads outlined across the interior's forests and plains.

In November, 1887, Punta Arenas' governor visited Liberia for the first time. Mr. Aguire had to admire the prospering colony, the wise measures taken to expand its resources, the complete fusion of different populations, and the order, ease, and happiness that reigned in every household. He examined the man who had accomplished such fine things, who was only known by the title Kaw-djer. He made free with compliments, saying:

"The Hosteian colony is your work, Mr. Governor, and Chile is glad to have given you the occasion to accomplish it."

"A treaty," replied Kaw-djer, "had placed this island, which belonged to itself, under Chilean rule, so it was right that Chile reestablished its independence."

Mr. Aguire understood the restrictive meaning of these words. Kaw-djer did not feel that the act of restitution meant that any thanks were owed to the Chilean government. Mr. Aguire, refusing to commit himself, said:

"In any cáse, I don't think *The Jonathan*'s emigrants can be missing the African land grants in Lagoa . . ."

"Indeed, Mr. Governor, because there they would be under Portuguese rule whereas here they answer to no one."

"So all is for the best?"

"For the best," replied Kaw-djer.

"We hope," Mr. Aguire continued, "that good relations between Chile and Hoste Island will continue."

"We hope so, too," said Kaw-djer, "and perhaps noting the results of the system applied at Hoste Island, the Chilean republic would be inclined to expand it to the Magellanic Archipelago's other islands?"

Mr. Aguire could not keep from smiling and did not reply, as he had nothing to say.

Mr. Rhodes, who was present at the discussion along with Messrs. O'Nark and Broks, understood that this subject could not be pursued. He did want, however, to draw the governor's attention to the current state of Ushaia colony, as opposed to Hoste Island.

"Mr. Aguire, you see," he said, "on one side is prosperity, on the other famine. With Argentina's coercive intervention, colonists refuse to come, ships refuse a port that is not free, which is a business necessity, and despite its governor's pleas, Ushaia is making no progress . . ."

"I agree," replied Mr. Aguire. "The Chilean government acted in an entirely different way with Punta Arenas. Without making the colony entirely independent, it can be granted many privileges that assure its future."

Mr. Rhodes had to admit that this observation was correct, although Kaw-djer doubtless would never admit it. Next he made a direct proposal about a project that could not be realized without the Chilean governor's accord.

"Mr. Governor," he said, "I would ask that Chile grant us possession of one of the archipelago's small islands, a heap of barren rocks, since this islet has no value."

"Which one?" asked Mr. Aguire.

"Cape Horn Islet."

"What would you want to do there?"

"Build a lighthouse, which is much needed at the tip of the American continent. Lighting the channels would be a big help for ships, not only those that come to Hoste Island or the channels of Navarin, Wollaston, Hermitte, and Tierra del Desolation, but also those wanting to round the cape between the Atlantic and the Pacific."

Messrs. Rhodes, O'Nark, and Broks, who were informed about Kaw-djer's project, backed up his request by arguing its real importance. After seeing the existing light at Terre des Etats, ships did not see a single one until the Chilean shore islands, at great peril to navigation.

Mr. Aguire realized that the proposal was well founded, and different governments had several times requested that a light be placed on the extreme tip of Cape Horn.

"So," he asked, "the Hoste Island colony would be ready to build this lighthouse?"

"Yes, Mr. Governor," replied Kaw-djer.

"At its own cost?"

"At its own cost, but under the strict condition that Chile grant her the entire ownership of Cape Horn Island."

Mr. Aguire promised to transmit the proposal to the president of the Chilean republic. The judicial branch would decide whether to pursue the plan.

When Mr. Aguire went back aboard the sloop that would take him to Punta Arenas, he could only congratulate himself once more. His government had to be satisfied by the Hosteian colony's prosperity, which guaranteed the future of its Magellanic possessions.

Three weeks later, Kaw-djer was informed that the proposal about Cape Horn Island and the Hoste Island colonists had been submitted for discussion in the Chilean chambers of justice. Sober debates ensued, and the proposal was accepted.

A land grant act was drafted, to be signed by the president of the republic and Hoste Island's governor, stating that the colony would build and maintain a lighthouse on the Cape's farthest tip.

The treaty between Chile and Hoste Island was signed on December 15, 1887.

Kaw-djer intended to complete this project without delay, and work had to start before the fine weather ended. It took two years to finish, and after that navigational safety was assured when approaching these dangerous waters.

XV

TROUBLE

The summer season ended with favorable climatic conditions. This seventh year since the colony was founded benefited from an exceptional harvest. New sawmills were built on the island's interior, some powered by steam, while others used electricity generated from waterfalls at the Yacana River's sources. Fisheries and canneries did a brisk business, and 3,775 tons of goods were shipped in and out of Liberia's port.

Winter interrupted the work begun at Cape Horn to build the lighthouse, the rooms where motors and dynamos would be installed to provide electrical energy. Cape Horn is around forty kilometers away from the Hardy Peninsula, and building material had to be transported with difficulty by sea across the Hermitte Island Channel, crowded with islets and reefs.

Winter's arrival brought particular worries for farmers about their five thousand head of livestock. It was impossible to let them wander around the campos; they needed food and shelter. Every precaution was taken, and resulting losses were minimal.

The winter season brought wind storms and violent tempests, but not excessive cold, and even in July, the temperature was never less than ten degrees below zero centigrade.

Liberia and the other two villages offered the comfort that shared prosperity had brought to every family. There was no poverty on Hoste Island, and there were no crimes against individuals or property. Occasional civil disputes occurred, and were settled by fair rulings from Kaw-djer and the administrative committee that worked alongside him.

It seemed that no trouble would ever threaten the colony, when toward the end of August, news arrived that could have been very serious, given the human vice of greed.

A gold deposit had been discovered on the northwest part of the island.

Learning this news, Kaw-djer had an ominous feeling that only worsened after further thought. He instinctively foresaw future misfortunes, and he discussed these the same day with Mr. Rhodes in his office.

The two wise men were in complete agreement on this point, that nothing good for the colony would come of this discovery.

"When our work is done," said Kaw-djer, "and all we have to do is gather the fruit of our efforts, luck, accursed luck throws the threat of disturbance and ruin into our colony . . . Yes, ruin, for the discovery of gold always brings ruin with it!"

"I agree with you, my friend," replied Mr. Rhodes, "and I fear that our community cannot resist this deadly influence. Farmers may abandon their fields, and workers their factories, in order to run to the placer mines."

"Gold, gold, the thirst for gold!" Kaw-djer repeated. "No worse plague could strike our colony!"

"Unfortunately," replied Mr. Rhodes, "we are unable to ward it off."

"No, my dear Rhodes. One can fight against an epidemic, eliminate and destroy it. But there is no remedy for gold fever, the most destructive agent of any social order. Can one doubt it after what happened in the gold mining districts of the Old and New World, in Australia, California, and South Africa? Useful work was abandoned from one day to the next, colonists deserted the fields and cities, families were divided over the lodes. And for most miners, the gold they mined with such greed was wasted in loathsome madness, like any easily gotten gain, and the poor got only misery from it."

Kaw-djer's vehement speech betrayed the degree of his concern.

"Not only is there danger from within," he added, "but also from outside, from adventurers and other lower orders who invade a country, disturbing and overthrowing it, in order to rip the accursed metal from its guts! They come from all corners of the earth! It's an avalanche that leaves only a void in its wake. Ah! Why must our island be threatened by such disaster?"

"Is there no hope left?" asked Mr. Rhodes. "If the news doesn't get around, maybe we'll be saved from invasion by foreigners."

"No," replied Kaw-djer, "it's already too late to prevent the evil from happening! It is unimaginable how quickly the entire world hears that gold deposits have been found in an area! It's as if the news were sent by air, and the winds brought this plague so contagious that all too often the finest and wisest of men are afflicted and succumb to it! It's horrible, and if I knew how to find a refuge outside our beloved and unfortunate island, I'd leave this minute . . ."

"Leave us," shouted Mr. Rhodes, grabbing Kaw-djer's hand as if to hold him back, "leave your duty at a moment of danger?"

The Kaw-djer did not reply. It was scarcely believable that a man so secure and energetic could be so emotionally shaken. Surely he didn't exaggerate, and the discovery would bring great harm to the colony. Finally, he got hold of himself. No! He wouldn't leave, he would do everything possible to confront the evil, and after that momentary lapse, he rose and for the first time pronounced these words, as if in spite of himself:

"May God help us!"

The discovery had been made on the morning of August 25 in the following manner:

On a hunt, Marc Rhodes and some of the colonists, after leaving Liberia around seven o'clock in a mail coach, went to within around twenty kilometers of the northwestern foothills of Hardy Peninsula.

A dense forest, not yet exploited, usually sheltered Hoste Island's animals, a handful of pumas and jaguars, which were better killed off because they preyed on sheep.

The hunters combed the forest, killing two pumas, and reached the other edge.

There, a large jaguar appeared, attempting to flee by climbing the slope of the hill. At this spot a torrential brook raged, which went round the forest and flowed into the Yacana River, past wet mud bristling with marine grasses.

Marc Rhodes noticed the animal and aimed, hitting him in the left side. The jaguar wasn't fatally wounded, and after a roar of anger rather than pain, he leapt toward the torrent and vanished into the woods.

A second shot was heard while the beast was fleeing. The bullet hit the rock at an angle, at the base of the hill, on the edge of the marsh and the stone flew into shards.

The hunters would have left the spot to continue chasing the jaguar, but one of the shards hit Marc Rhodes slightly, and he curiously examined it and saved it.

It was a piece of quartz with typical veins, in which some gold particles were easily recognized.

Gold! There was gold in the soil at Hoste Island! The only evidence of it was that rock shard. Was it such a surprise? Lodes of precious metals had been revealed at Brunswick Island, around Punta Arenas, as well as in Tierra del Fuego, in Patagonia as well as Magellania. Gold washers had spread over the surface of these territories like vermin gnawing at them. From Alaska to Cape Horn, a gold chain enriches the spinal chord of the two Americas, which in four centuries have yielded forty-five billion francs.

Marc Rhodes understood the seriousness of this discovery. He would have preferred to keep it a secret, only telling his father who would inform Kaw-djer. But he was not the only one to know it. His hunting companions had examined the piece of rock and collected other shards that also contained gold particles.

The secret was out, and that same day the entire island knew they would be the envy of the archipelago's other islands. It was like a trail of gunpowder that a spark could set ablaze, running from Liberia to the other villages.

First, everyone thought that possibly the gold deposits were not only in the marsh area at the foot of the hill and the edge of the brook. New searches might reveal gold elsewhere. Prospectors would come from everywhere in Magellania, digging into and turning over soil previously used only for farming. Unsociable adventurers with names and origins unknown, apart from the nicknames they called one another, would rush to the island. They would try to discover new places, fight with the colonists to chase them off their land, and even fight with their companions, always ready to rob and tear one another apart. Could Tom Land's well-organized men, the island militia, disarm these marauding hordes?

Since the first traces of gold were discovered at Golden Creek—that was the little Yakana River tributary's name—the most avid Liberians went there, despite the best efforts of Kaw-djer and his friends to hold them back. Several hundred colonists, abandoning their homes, factories, and fields, leaving work unfinished, hurried to the lodes and found rich veins in the quartz rocks.

As good administrators, Kaw-djer and his council had to intervene to organize the exploitation and maintain order, no matter what they thought of it. They even considered making the yields of the lodes common property, and extract the gold for the benefit of the colony in a way to share the profits equally among everyone. But from the first day, they were overwhelmed. Each man wanted to work for his own benefit, hoping to find a full pocket, a valuable nugget, and unearth fortune with a pick, and all wise advice was ignored.

To work the placers, there were no material difficulties. All one had to do was to attack the rock with a pick, and break it into bits to extract the gold particles. Moreover, the muddy marshland near Golden Creek was easily worked, and it sufficed to establish claims where it washed up to collect the metal brought along with it.

It is known that gold-bearing lands are most often composed of mud washed down by winter ice, thinned with water, sifted and filtered through the soil. They came from erosion after heavy rains and the disintegration of quartz worn down by the torrents. All the equipment needed was a plate to collect the mud, and a little water to wash it. With this rudimentary equipment, from the start, colonists obtained gold for a sum that varied from day to day and according to the individual from 150 to 500 francs.

On the Golden Creek placer, a layer of mud five feet deep by thirty to forty feet wide produced nine or ten plates per cubic foot, and it was very rare that each washing did not yield gold in particles or nuggets. The nuggets were only like grains of sand, so these claims, whose size was mentioned above, would not produce twenty million francs as they do in other regions.

The Golden Creek placers did not yield this much from the beginning, of course; others were observed in the area that rendered large profits. People's fascination grew from day to day. An irresistible madness emptied Liberia of most families—men, women, and children—who all went to work on the claims. Some hit it rich by discovering in the interstices of rocks a pocket or nuggets that accumulated as a result of torrential rain. Even those who worked for long days with great fatigue and no results did not lose hope. But everyone came, not only from the capital, but from other deserted villages, trading posts, fisheries, and coastal factories. Soon only about a hundred colonists remained in Liberia, faithful to their homes, families, and businesses, but severely tested by the current situation. The gold seemed to possess a magnetic power, which the human mind could not resist.

Even though Kaw-djer did not let himself go for a single instant, showing an energy that never flagged, his friends noticed that he looked deeply discouraged. No wonder, since he was a man who had never been governed by passions, except the passion to do good. He spent his whole life concentrated on this ideal, sacrificing everything for it. Now, after having reconnected to humanity by so many ties, and returned after such a long separation, humanity appeared to him with all its faults, dishonor, and vice! His work would crumble, and ruins would abound in the unfortunate colony, because chance made some gold particles shoot out of a rock shard!

Mr. Rhodes, trying to react against his insurmountable disgust, told him:

"It can't last . . .The lodes will run out . . . The colonists will go back to their lives as before . . ."

"And if it's too late!" he replied.

The attempts by Kaw-djer and his friends to restrain the Hosteian population failed, as did the Anglican and Catholic missionaries. Fathers Athanase and Severin in their church and the Allen Gordon Mission's ministers in theirs preached sermons in vain against the gold madness as revealing deplorable appetites, full of future disappointments! They were unheeded and soon not a single churchgoer attended sermons any more.

As painful and sad as it may be to admit, only the Indians, among Hoste Island inhabitants, knew how to avoid getting carried away like the rest. They alone did not give themselves up to insane greed. All praise and honor is due to these humble Fuegians for keeping several farms and fisheries active; their honest natures, inspired by the missionaries, kept them from such excesses. These poor people still obeyed Kaw-djer, their benefactor; they recalled all he had done for them, and almost all remained as faithful as Halg and Karroly.

Had the discovery been limited to the Golden Creek lodes, perhaps the claims would have been quickly exhausted. The colonists, mostly disappointed, would have gone back to their usual tasks in the fields and towns. But other lodes were found in the southwest of the island, near Rous Point, as rich and easier to work.

Prospectors by the thousand hurried to this side, scarcely able to provide the basic necessities for living there. At these places, greedy men fighting for ownership of placers, were almost homeless, exposed to the often stormy weather during the warm season, with marsh air thick with foul-smelling odors and insalubrious mud, and soon illness and poverty assailed them.

Their numbers grew every day. As it had happened in other countries, foreigners flooded into the island. Crews deserted their ships to run to the lodes. Barely anchored in Liberia's port, the ships were abandoned and captains disobeyed, and sometimes even officers set an example by deserting. The already varied Hoste Island population was augmented by sailors of every nationality, British, Danes, Norwegians, Americans, and Germans, many of them adventurers who would stop at nothing and who knew only one law, that of brute force. What were they doing at Liberia? Ships sent to pick up building wood, livestock, grain, and furs had nothing to load. The cargo stores were exhausted after the first week. The future continually worried Kaw-djer and he had to intervene energetically to prevent the export of grain and canned goods, which would have exposed the colony to the full horror of famine. Although he could check this evil somewhat, he remained powerless against the poverty that continued to grow since the villages and countryside had been abandoned.

Toward the end of January, the chaos reached a frightful level. Joining the colonists and deserters in swarming over the lodes were gold washers who ran from different parts of the Magellanic Archipelago, and Patagonian territories, and we know how numerous they are! The richest vein in the world is the cordillera that develops in faraway regions of Alaska, and crosses the United States, Mexico, Colombia, the Equator, Peru, Bolivia, Chile, and Argentina up to the last outbranching of Cape Horn, which has still not been exhausted. Exaggeration played its role, stirring Old and New Worlds people to call Hoste Island an extraordinary pocket, an island made of gold, where the richest treasures of the chain were piled up. No surprise then, that the lower orders that raced to California, Australia, Southern Africa, and a few years later to the Alaskan Klondike [Gold was discovered there in 1896; Verne describes the bad results in *The Golden Volcano*], also invaded Hoste Island!

Perhaps the Chilean government regretted abandoning Hoste Island to *The Jonathan*'s castaways. Soon they had precise information from Punta Arenas' governor. It was necessary to use restraint, and it could be predicted that by working the island's placers, more people would be ruined than enriched!

Nevertheless, toward the end of January, Kaw-djer estimated that over twenty thousand foreigners gathered in certain places, where they would eventually devour one other. What could be expected from these madmen, already engaged in bloody battles for ownership of claims, when famine pitted them against one another?

Tom Land and Karroly kept Kaw-djer updated about events, both men heedless of fatigue and danger. Kaw-djer also didn't hesitate to put his life on the line. He went to Rous Point, where his friends followed. Anglican ministers and Catholic missionaries also went. He threw himself in the middle of the mob to stop the violence. It was useless. The dregs of every nation didn't know him, and his colonists no longer knew him. His intervention almost ended badly for him. He was pushed, threatened, and nearly lost his life for carrying out his duty.

Kaw-djer returned to Liberia, desperate and sickened by all this abomination, and his entourage began to think of the possibility of abandoning Hoste Island.

Before going to this extreme step, Messrs. Rhodes, Broks, and O'Nark and some others discussed whether to ask the Chilean government for help. Tom Land's militia, already reduced by desertions, was powerless, so he agreed this was the only way to stop the chaos.

"The Chilean government cannot abandon us," said Mr. Rhodes. "It's in their own interest that the colony calms down."

"An appeal to foreigners!" shouted Kaw-djer.

"Only one of the Punta Arenas war ships," said Mr. Broks, "need sail in view of the island, and these wretches will soon be driven away . . ."

"Let Karroly leave for Punta Arenas," Mr. O'Nark, "and within fifteen days . . ."

"No!" said Kaw-djer. "No! We made ourselves! We can save ourselves!"

They could only accede to his categorical will, worthy of the man's great character.

Kaw-djer stayed at his post although it was no longer possible to act as governor, and aided by a young doctor—Mr. Rhodes' son-in-law—the benefactor devoted himself to the sick, whose number increased every day.

Indeed, Hoste Island was stricken by an epidemic caused by poverty and excesses of all kinds. Thanks to unremitting zeal and informed care, most of the sick were saved from death, apart from a few hundred victims, out of a total of twenty thousand prospectors.

Finally, toward the end of March, there was a kind of calming of the widespread madness. The lodes ran out, and for every few rich men who benefited from luck, there were many impoverished people, who lost their last piastre, their health, and their futures. Even these few fortunes were lost as it inevitably happens, in gaming houses and underground gambling dens where revolver shots drowned out the players' shouts. Liberia was spared such scenes, but they were all too frequent in the other two towns.

The various claims at Hardy Peninsula and Rous Point produced three million francs' worth of gold. At nearby Nassau Bay the production was so minimal that it was almost immediately abandoned. In any case, the gold didn't profit the colonists, falling instead into the hands of adventurers that Europe and mainly America had thrown onto Hoste Island.

Finally, this heap of people who had lost their social position, this rabble left this corner of the Magellanic Archipelago, where so much lay in ruins. The unfortunate Hosteian families, mostly decimated, hounded by poverty, and voraciously hungry, returned to Liberia. There they found all the help Kaw-djer could offer, and the tireless devotion, which he had shown so many times during these awful troubles.

Could the colony survive such a blow? After having been deeply discouraged, would Kaw-djer rediscover his former energy and would his hand be powerful enough to move on to a new reorganization?

Would he wish to do so? His friends feared that after so many disappointments, and finding himself face to face with all the vices of humanity, he might want to leave Hoste Island.

However, devoting oneself to the work of repair was a noble task, worthy of a great mind. After having saved them once from the excesses of anarchy, Kaw-djer was moved to go back to work, to restore the colony that had been his, and which he had made so prosperous.

Some days went by before his intentions became clear. He remained shut up in his home, not speaking to anyone, or wandered alone over the heights of Hardy Peninsula, and on the highest rocks, would stay motionless for long hours, looking to the south as he had before.

Perhaps his thoughts brought him back to the tip of the continent at Cape Horn, on the rock whose independence he had obtained. Would that become a refuge where Karroly would take him to continue the solitary life they lived at New Island?

Liberia regained its liveliness little by little. Stores opened again. Mr. Rhodes and his friends did their best to raise the colonists' spirits, obtaining supplies for them, and put them back on the right path amid the ruins. It was as if a horrible cyclone had devastated the island; its inhabitants were stricken as if a meteor had fallen on their heads. There was no fear of such ordeals happening again. The ground was drained of all the gold it had possessed. It had been searched to the depths of its entrails. Now it was necessary to produce wood, grain, and grass again, to provide food for those who lived from the soil, and not bits of metal whose discovery had caused such disaster!

Finally, after several days of absence, Kaw-djer gathered his friends, collaborators, and others who so often appreciated his help. In a low but firm voice in which all the old energy could be felt, he said:

"To work!"

XVI

THE CAPE HORN LIGHTHOUSE

Winter was coming. How would the stricken island survive the threat of famine, with part of its population still dispersed in the interior? True, all the foreigners had left, since nothing remained for them to take.

Had they only taken gold, there might have been less regret. For a country's wealth is not measured by its gold deposits, but by the fertility of its soil, its business and industry, which are all generally lacking in gold regions. Before the Golden Creek placer was found, the colony enjoyed an enviable prosperity, with equal prospects for the future.

But misfortune struck. Factories, fisheries, and forest mills were abandoned. It was the height of disaster that farmers left their fields and many animals died from lack of care, left by themselves in the middle of pasturelands; the soil was not planted and the next season's harvest was irremediably lost.

Most essential was to prevent famine with winter about to cover the whole Magellanic Archipelago with snow and ice. Firewood was scarce in Liberia and the two other towns of Rous Point and Nassau Bay, and protection was needed against the cold as well as against hunger.

In a meeting held on April third, at his home, Kaw-djer declared:

"We can only ensure our colony's health by hard work, which will succeed only if everyone participates and is resigned to it. We can only count upon ourselves to get out of this situation, and first of all, we must tally the island's resources."

"We'll do it," replied Mr. Rhodes, "and we'll support you for the common good. I hope there will be no disagreement between the colonists and ourselves! They are so stricken and miserable that they realize they must submit without recriminations or protests to your authority. Act as a determined leader, who explains his orders, and who shall be obeyed by all. We have full confidence in you, your energy, and practical mind. We know you have no personal ambition. You only follow the road of duty, and we follow you on it . . ."

"And if you need unlimited powers," added Mr. Broks, "go right ahead and take them!"

Kaw-djer understood what the colony's current condition required. To rise to the circumstances, which were so bleak, it was necessary to act as a master or dictator, and he knew that the dictator had to be him.

Mr. O'Nark drew his friends' attention to the following point:

"When the chaos was at its height, with possessions and people at the utmost risk, when we suffered attacks from foreigners, fearsome by their number and audacity, we thought of asking for help from Chile . . ."

"And I was against it," shouted Kaw-djer. "That might have compromised Hoste Island's independence, and I would never agree to sacrifice even the smallest part of that!"

"We agreed with you," declared Mr. Rhodes. "Our colony must remain free, and if we go back to Chilean rule, we abandon freedom with no hope of regaining it."

"We are agreed on the subject," continued Mr. O'Nark, "and Hoste Island must belong only to itself. But without alienating its rights in any way . . ."

"What are you getting at?" asked Kaw-djer.

"If the Chilean government offered its help now, not to restore order, but to supply our most pressing needs, we should accept, and even call upon . . ."

"I agree," replied Kaw-djer, "on the express condition that these contacts with the Chilean republic can in no case give them any claims on the island . . ."

"That's how we feel," agreed Mr. Rhodes, "and even were it a question of protectorate, we'd refuse . . ."

"Our flag and only our flag," Kaw-djer declared, "and I will not allow it to be lowered for any other!"

And in a ringing voice he shouted:

"Long live an independent Hoste Island!"

From this day on, Kaw-djer's authority was unlimited, and not one discordant note was heard in the entire colony. He could never admit that man should bear the yoke of an absolute master, but he was that master, and because of him, Hoste Island would rise from the ruins.

The colonists understood that a single hand should direct everything. Kaw-djer's first task was to proceed with a detailed inquiry on each family's resources, and what was left after the pillaging of the island's stored goods. Without favoring anyone, a rationing system would be set up while awaiting the arrival of grain that would be enough until the next harvest. Kaw-djer had the difficult task of feeding three thousand inhabitants during winter, when death had claimed most of the livestock, and grain was reduced to a few hundred quintals [One quintal = 100 kg.].

From the beginning, the indispensable rationing set off some attempts at rebellion. The need to surrender what they still possessed for the common good was badly received by some families, who were obliged to give up more than they got back in shared property. But these were necessary measures and Kaw-djer's orders were executed rigorously. Tom Land was once again director of the reorganized colonial police, which went after anyone who refused to submit to sharing for the common good. After making a few examples of people, Kaw-djer, backed by public opinion, conquered the last resisters.

Supply duty was organized to gather the necessary firewood in the capital and other towns. At the end of April, the cold got worse, even though the winter temperature was no lower than usual. Although the thermometer did not dip measurably, the Hosteians suffered considerably from the humidity, due to abundant rain and snow. The wood for winter had to be gathered from the forests, and the job consisted in felling trees, cutting them up, and transporting them to places where they would be used.

Trips were also organized to collect livestock from farms for work in the towns. Five or six hundred animals were gathered, most of which were used to feed the colony.

Requests were made of Chile, Argentina, and the Falklands, about seeding the fields in September and repopulating the ovine and bovine animals, which would be replaced at this time in the pasturelands when the last snows disappeared. Three or four months would go by before the Magellanic Archipelago's channels were navigable for coastal trade. It was clear that the colony was dependent on its reserves. Rationing was a necessity. Individual interests had to cede to the general good.

In July, winter was felt at its harshest. But because of the preparations, there was enough fuel and the worst cold was fought off without too much trouble. The rough weather did not impede Kaw-djer's reorganization project. He wanted to see and even do everything himself. Visits to villages, trips to the island's interior at different places on the shore, trading posts, factories, and fisheries constantly put him into contact with the population. It seemed as if he had taken up his previous life when he traveled through the Fuegian territory, going from tribe to tribe and campground to campground, deserving the fine name and title of benefactor. Age had not lessened any of his stamina or activity, and on Hoste Island he rediscovered the popularity he had won among the small Indian tribes.

His friends aided him bravely. Heedless of fatigue, they accompanied him, giving their help with total devotion. Mr. Rhodes' son-in-law was busy doctoring in Liberia, so Kaw-djer took up his medical duties once again and replaced him in the villages and the countryside.

Karroly was always by Kaw-djer's side, as the bad weather gave him time off from piloting. The devoted friend followed his master everywhere, while Halg stayed near his young wife who had just given birth, busying himself with hunting and fishing.

Finally winter ended at the beginning of October, and the archipelago emerged from its snowy covering in the heat of the sun rising toward the equator. The first ships appeared from the Falklands and Chile; cargoes arrived at Liberia's storehouses, and famine was no longer a danger.

"Just in time," said Kaw-djer to Mr. Rhodes. "Another month, and we would have run out of reserves! By the end of the week, there would have been no more bread. Now we have nothing to fear . . ."

"Thanks to you, my friend," replied Mr. Rhodes, "and your farsighted and energetic administration. Allow us to express our gratitude . . ."

"Your gratitude?" replied Kaw-djer. "You deserve the entire colony's thanks for the devotion you've shown, but let's be satisfied with having done our duty . . ."

"So be it," continued Mr. Rhodes, who doubtless wished to speak his mind, feeling that the moment had come. "But also, my friend, we must thank God for having put you on our path, to save *The Jonathan*'s castaways, and to save our island . . ."

"God?" murmured Kaw-djer, his eyes raised almost involuntarily to heaven.

All the work involving industry, business, and agriculture that could not be done during the winter season was now addressed. Liberia regained all its previous liveliness. Business deals were made with new energy. The port received more vessels, with no threat of their crews' deserting. Whale hunting became productive in the Magellanic waters and in Hoste Island's neighboring channels. For this purpose, Americans and Norwegians flooded into Liberia's port, and one hundred Hosteians worked at high salaries manufacturing whale oil. The capital's storehouses filled with imported merchandise, and other goods for ships to take on coastal trading and long voyages.

At the same time, factories, sawmills, and canneries became active again; the number of sea lion hunters doubled. Several hundred Pecherais, abandoning Tierra del Fuego where Argentina's hand weighed too heavily upon them, permanently moved their campgrounds to the island's shore. Other colonists, mostly from Canada and North America, were brought by emigration companies, and they tripled the Hosteian population.

Two years went by, and thanks to Kaw-djer's government, there was no longer any trace of the upheavals caused by the discovery of gold deposits. The colony's importance was measured by trade figures of several million piastres. A second port was established above Nassau Bay; its tip was washed by the waters of Beagle Canal, which presented excellent navigability up to the Magellan Straits. Commercial relations with Punta Arenas became more frequent, enriching both capitals. Salesmen would have found the same advantages at Ushaia, had the Argentinean colony benefited from the free port status granted to its rivals, which ensured their amazing prosperity.

Several Hosteian homes lodged coastal traders, who trafficked to the east with the Falklands, to the west with the Chilean islands. Along the shore they collected all the island-manufactured products, not only at the two villages of Nassau Bay and Rous Point, but also those founded on the Gordon Island narrows and the entrance to Darwin Sound. The latest census attributed to Hoste Island a population of five thousand inhabitants, one-sixth of them Indians.

Toward the end of 1890, the colony purchased a three hundred-ton-steamer from the Chilean government, built at Valparaiso. The steamer was given the name *Yacana*. It would be used for the colony's dealings with the archipelago's different trading posts, and the governor's frequent trips to various shore enterprises. But Kaw-djer never set foot on any of the islands given by the 1881 treaty to one or another of the two republics.

At this time, in the middle of the fine season, work was finished on a metal pylon fifty years high, whose lantern was six hundred feet above sea level, at the farthest tip of Cape Horn; at the base of the cape were the annexes where the dynamos were installed to produce electric current, housing for the keepers, and all the equipment needed for a first-class lighthouse to function.

It was decided to celebrate the opening of the lighthouse, with a memorable ceremony for the colonists. The entire population could not attend since the transportation between Hoste Island and Horn Island was limited. The colony's notables would be present, however.

Kaw-djer wrote his invitations accordingly, and opening day was set for January 15, 1891. The steamer *Yacana* carried the governor's guests, council members and others, and their families, not to mention Karroly and his son, justly considered Hoste Island notables.

Sea traders from the port and other small boats able to make the crossing accompanied the steamer.

Around eleven o'clock in the morning of the fifteenth, the *Yacana* left Liberia's port, after taking aboard about one hundred passengers, men and women. It followed the Hardy Peninsula to its tip, escorted by a dozen small boats.

The weather was favorable for the trip, as the wind blew from the northeast, across the arms of sea and channel up to Cape Horn.

About ten nautical leagues as the crow flies separated Hardy Peninsula and the farthest island of the archipelago.

The flotilla made its way without accident or delay, sheltered by high land. The *Yacana* did not even need to slow down its pace, and the small boats were still in sight of the Hosteian flag waving at its gaff.

After having turned past Hardy Peninsula, the steamer headed for the northern tip of Hermitte Island, and after reaching this spot, left it to starboard in order to enter the channel that opened onto the sea to the west of the cape.

Horn Island was reached around 3:00 P.M. The steamer dropped anchor at the back of a cove where, during the storm, the *Wel-kiej* went to the aid of *The Jonathan*, and the small boats cast off their moorings.

Around 150 people debarked with Kaw-djer. They landed on a beach, framed by blackish reefs and strewn with gleaming seashells, which followed a gentle slope to the base of the cape. Workers were waiting who put the final touches on the lighthouse; they were often in contact with Karroly when the longboat brought Kaw-djer there before the *Yacana* had been acquired by the colony.

As soon as he set foot on shore, Kaw-djer headed for the path that led up the side of the foreland. His friends let him go, understanding that he wanted to be alone. Mr. Rhodes, his wife and children, and the families of Messrs. Broks and O'Nark began a visit of the annexes guided by the lighthouse keepers.

Kaw-djer climbed slowly, without turning his head, absorbed in his thoughts as ten years before, when after leaving New Island, he fled to the farthest lands of the continent.

Arriving at the foreland's summit, he stopped for a moment. Then, covering the twenty steps that separated him from the crest, he stood there motionless.

He recalled his past life, his studious youth, his mature years spent fighting for his ideas, the disdain he developed for humanity, followed by his breaking off with his fellow man, his life amid the Magellanic Archipelago's Indians, his move to New Island, which he thought would be a permanent one, the calm years with Karroly, then the treaty that expelled him from his refuge, his arrival at Cape Horn, *The Jonathan*'s shipwreck, and finally his stay on Hoste Island . . .

He had greatly changed since he threw his former theories to the winds, when he devoted himself to organizing the new colony! Was he still the man whose doctrine was summed up by the loathsome formula: "Neither God nor master!"

No, on this rock, he spoke the following word with an irresistible burst of faith:

"God!"

At that moment, he saw a pile of stones at the edge of the plateau, debris that had been removed to lay the lighthouse's foundations.

One of the stones attracted his particular attention. It balanced on the edge of the plateau, and a nudge from his toe would have sent it to be swallowed up by the cape waters.

Kaw-djer approached. His eyes had a fiery gleam, a flame of contempt and hatred . . .

He was correct; the stone, striped with shining lines, contained gold, perhaps an entire fortune that the workers had not noticed. It lay there, abandoned like a worthless lump. So the new continent's long chain projected its gold-bearing outbranchings up to Cape Horn, and the rock's bowels harbored more precious metal.

Kaw-djer saw again all the disasters that struck Hoste Island after the Golden Creek lode's discovery, the colony's panic, the invasion by adventurers from every corner of the world, followed by famine, poverty, and ruin.

Then, he kicked the enormous nugget away with his foot.

"Begone, accursed gold," he shouted, "and with you may all humanity's evils be drowned!"

The stone rolled and bounded off the rock's ledge, disappearing in the depths of the sea at the foot of the foreland.

A few moments later, following a sign from Kaw-djer, passengers from the *Yacana* and the small boats climbed the slope and reached the plateau.

On that day at sunset, the lighthouse was to be lit for the first time. It was constructed of a perforated iron armature, which was protected from winds, a pylon whose lantern rose fifty feet above the plateau, which brought it to 1,800 feet above sea level.

Kaw-djer and his friends, all invited to the opening ceremony, were lined up around the pylon.

Mr. Rhodes spoke a few emotional words, addressing Kaw-djer, and through him the entire colony showed their gratitude and affection for the one who had done so much for them. He evoked what had happened ten years before when the storm blew the disabled *Jonathan* into the coastline; he mentioned what happened on Hoste Island, when no less disabled than the vessel, the colony was nearly a victim of anarchy, and then of foreign invasion.

After Mr. Rhodes' eloquent words, there came shouts from all sides:

"Long live Kaw-djer! Long live Kaw-djer!" and the latter merely raised his hand to the sky in reply.

The cheers were continuing with patriotic ardor, when a flag with the Hosteian colors unfurling in the wind was hoisted to the top of the lighthouse.

They went down to the shore around five o'clock to partake of a meal served in the annex's main dining room and there enthusiastic toasts were drunk to the colony's prosperity and Kaw-djer's honor.

Dinner was over a little after seven o'clock, and all present returned to the foreland's summit, wanting to be there when the first luminous rays shone across space.

The sun hovered above the western horizon. The sky was revealed in all its purity, and the dying breeze did not carry a single cloud along with it.

Deep silence reigned, with an underlying emotion that they all shared. They looked toward the immense sector already darkened in the east, while the sunset still purpled the horizon. Not a sail was seen on the expanse of sea, no smoke wafted on the perimeter of the deserted immensity.

The sun touched the horizon. Enlarged by refraction, it was soon reduced to a semicircle, whose last beams illuminated the sky, and then, only a glowing strip that was engulfed by the water.

It gave off a luminous green light, complementary in color to the red that had gone.

At this moment, the current sent from below made an electric arc shoot out between the lantern's plugs, whose beam projected through the lenticular glass to all points on the horizon.

The lighthouse had just thrown its first beams on Magellanic waters, and the *Yacana*'s two cannons saluted it by firing amid endless applause from the spectators.

Now a vessel coming from the east—after having seen the light at Ile des Etats at the tip of the Fuegian coastline—could sight the Cape Horn lighthouse, built by Hoste Island's colonists at the juncture of the Atlantic and Pacific Oceans, before observing lights on Chilean waters.